To Catch A Feather

R. A. Hutchins

ISBN: 9798745930218

For Michael

and my Mam and Dad,

Who are all the Wind beneath my Wings,

Love you xxx

CONTENTS

Then

Now

Then

ONE

Kate sat back against the smooth, weather-beaten stone and let the wind rush over her, drying her tears just as quickly as more fell to replace them. She looked out over the North Sea, grey and foreboding on this cold February day. It was welcoming in its bleak anger, the waves whipping up and over the pier below. She had seen it in all its moods, this natural beauty, from the turquoise peace of a summer's day to the most violent of storms, crashing against the rocks below. Here, from the shelter of the ancient priory at her back, she was merely an observer to its rage. And yet it set her free. Free from the emotions which tormented her thoughts. Free from the guilt of tasks incomplete. And more. Most importantly, free from the suffocation of sitting with her own thoughts at home.

Home. Kate wasn't sure where that was any more. Was it the small flat she shared with her best friend, Sal? Was it back with her parents in their 1960s bungalow? Or with her church family, on one of her increasingly infrequent visits to Sunday services? Kate sighed as the thoughts flitted through her head, an image of each place providing a fleeting question. None gave the answer she desired. Then there was Patrick – Rick to those who knew him well – his image hung longer than the others. His boyish grin and freckles. His unruly hair. Kate managed a small smile. The face of the man she was to marry never failed to give her a momentary feeling of warmth, of happiness perhaps.

Happiness. Another illusive notion. Kate couldn't remember the last time she had felt joy. Real, jump up and down and clap your hands wildly joy. The kind that bubbles up without restraint and infects all those around you. She had tried of course, but it was like catching a feather on the breeze. Illusive. Kate tried to think back to the last time she had registered the emotion. Any emotion, in fact, other than numb resignation or acute despair. The only moment that had come close was when Rick had proposed at her surprise thirtieth birthday party last August. She had been happy, then, hadn't she? Kate couldn't be sure. Not because the question hadn't pleased her, not because she hadn't said yes immediately, but rather because she seemed incapable of feeling happiness, even at one of the most important moments of her life. Rick had grinned with relief, taking her in his arms and kissing her passionately. Her parents had been excited at the prospect of seeing her wed, and of course her friends had begun speaking of wedding preparations excitedly. But Kate. Kate had kissed Rick back, nodded and smiled at everyone else, allowing inspection of her beautiful ring to fill the spaces where conversation should have flowed. In private later that night, she had prayed for God to release the hold of the anxiety and depression which held her heart in their claws. Her personal demons, Kate had battled them for most of her life. At times they were like old friends, annoyingly familiar and requesting her attention. At other times, like this past year, they became harsh taskmasters, directing her thoughts and actions, dictating her responses and her emotions. Kate felt like a puppet in their game.

She ran her hands through her windswept curls distractedly, pulling her scarf tighter about her face and sighed audibly. There was no one else here on this bitterly cold day, and Kate fished in the pockets of her woollen coat for the gloves she kept there. She was meeting Rick in an hour and needed to pull herself together. Wiping her nose and eyes ineffectually on her very damp tissue, Kate watched a seagull dipping and diving out on the waves far below. *How would it feel?* she wondered. *How would it feel to be set free, to just go away and ride whatever waves came her way?* The prospect was not an unattractive one, and Kate deliberately chose not to pursue the thought further. It would do no good, and would only serve to upset her further. The chains that trapped her were internal, not external. Where she ran, they would too, adding weight to her every step. No, Kate would meet Rick shortly in their favourite coffee shop, she would go to work tomorrow morning, in the vet's surgery where she was a nurse, and neither her fiancé nor her colleagues would be any the wiser to her personal torment.

TWO

Rick hovered at the top of the main street, beside the large, ornate fountain, wringing his hands. He knew that Kate would be there already, waiting patiently at their usual table, a cup of mint tea in front of her, teabag still in the cup. He knew her, what she liked to drink, her favourite books and music, even how her freshly-washed hair smelt. And yet, here he was, feeling as if he were about to meet a stranger. Increasingly indifferent to life and to him, Kate didn't seem to be bothered whether they met up or not these days. Between the start of the year and now, the couple had seen each other only three times. When Rick stopped initiating their dates, he had found that Kate made no comment. She didn't share any suggestions of her own, didn't text to say she was missing him. Nothing. If anything, she had shrunk further into her shell.

Not wanting to live together until married, Rick had hoped that their intimacy might increase at least a little after their engagement. More times spent getting to know each other in private rather than at the cinema or in restaurants. But, if anything, the opposite had been true. Kate had even declined to spend Christmas with him and his family back in Ireland. And that had been the final straw. So now he trudged with heavy feet and a heavier heart, along to meet his fiancée. The last time he could probably think of her as that, Rick noted morosely.

The heat of the small café hit him as he walked in, adding to his not inconsiderable discomfort. Rick ordered his usual caramel latte and headed to the far corner, where Kate sat observing him whilst blowing the steam from her cup. Her red curls were in disarray and Rick swallowed the lump that had formed in his throat at the sight of her.

"Hey," Kate said, half-standing to accept his peck on the cheek.

"Hey, you," Rick replied, shrugging out of his winter coat and taking the chair opposite. "How's it going?" He noted her swollen, blotchy face but made no comment.

"Oh, fine," Kate gave her stock answer, "You?"

Rick could hardly bare the pleasantries. He had better conversations with his aged aunt. As his coffee arrived, and the owner, Dan, provided a brief distraction, Rick decided that blunt was best.

"So, Katie," he said, using the term of endearment that he had created for her early in their relationship, then immediately regretting it, "I guess we need to talk." It was unoriginal, he knew, but he had nothing else, nothing better to lead with.

Kate's ears pricked up at that. His tone, his demeanour, were different from the easy-going man she was used to. Her heart began to beat a funeral chant in her chest. Kate had been here before. Not engaged, but her previous long-term boyfriend, Chris, had broken up with her after three years, stating he wanted to travel. He'd moved as far as York and taken up with the worship leader at his new church there. Within the year they were married and expecting their first child. What he'd meant by 'travel', Kate had deduced, was to get away from her. From her melancholy. Looking up into the eyes that were so familiar, yet so distant, Kate braced herself for the worst.

"How do you feel things are going? With us, I mean?" Rick rushed the sentence, keen to begin the conversation and reach its inevitable conclusion.

"How do you feel things are?" Kate expertly turned the question back to him. She was adept at avoidance.

"Well, I, I'm…" Rick struggled to find the words, realising too late that he should have practised this more. Written it out and learnt it by heart, perhaps. But even the thought of saying it, had grieved him such that he'd put it off till this moment. "I'm not feeling so close to you anymore." *Had he ever?* Rick wondered silently. There, he'd said it. Well, not quite said it, but it was a start.

"Oh?" Kate looked back at him enquiringly, her head tilted to one side, her face masking the inner turmoil which made her feel as if she were about to vomit.

She said nothing further, and Rick was forced to expand. Sighing heavily, he reached across to where her hands cradled her cup, and took one between his own, larger palms. "When we first met," he began cautiously, "things were great, weren't they? We met up a few times a week for dates, we talked for hours in this very coffee shop. We… shared things. Our hopes, our lives." He paused and looked Kate straight in the eye. It was she who turned away first. "But over the past six months, since we got engaged, you've become… distant." He raised an eyebrow speculatively, expecting a response. A denial.

Anything.

They sat in awkward silence for seconds which stretched into minutes. Finally, pulling her hand out of his, Kate spoke in a whisper, "Say it, Rick, say it and put us both out of this misery!"

Rick swallowed the emotion coiled in his throat. Did he really want to do this? Once spoken, the words could not be unsaid. He looked into the watery green eyes of the woman he loved. The woman he still loved.

Kate returned his gaze, wishing she could explain that her anxiety, held in check until last Summer by a combination of medication and CBT strategies, had been sent into overdrive as a result of a natural flare-up and then the pressure of others' expectations. His included. Talk of setting a date, making huge life choices, had weighed heavily on her mind and her chest until she was suffocated. Her doctor had suggested a change in regime, and the new prescription had, of course, come with side effects – Kate felt numb most of the time, to her anxiety, yes, but it was so much more than that. She was desensitized to life itself. When she wasn't distant and unreachable, even to herself, she was filled with an anguish so acute, it felt like a storm raging inside her, drowning all rational thought. She would not inflict herself on others, and so had retreated from friends and fiancé alike.

"I love you." Rick's whispered words released the flow which had barely been held in check up to this point, and Kate could not help herself. The tears streamed down her face. His hands found hers again and squeezed gently, Rick's thumbs rubbing a path around her palm. "I love you." He said it louder this time, his eyes never leaving hers.

"I love you, too," Kate whispered, seeing his shoulders visibly relax as he heard the truth in her words.

"Thank you," Rick could think of nothing else to say. It was what he had needed to hear. That she was not indifferent to him. It was a start. "Listen, Katie, let's not think of the wedding anymore."

"You want to break off the engagement?"

"What? No! I'm just saying that we need to shift our focus for a bit. To us. The two of us. Together."

"Oh, okay." Kate scrubbed at her wet cheeks with her free hand. Rick took his hands back and they both took a moment to regroup, sipping their drinks thoughtfully.

"Let's go away," Rick began, having clearly come to a

decision, the determination etched now in his sombre expression.

"Away?"

"It's half term in two weeks, I don't have much marking or preparation to do. Let's go away!" Rick held his breath, watching as Kate's thoughts flitted across her features.

"But we aren't married!" she whispered.

"Oh, come on, Katie! We're not in Victorian England, your reputation isn't at stake! We can get separate rooms if it'll make you feel better!" He tried, and failed, to not let his exasperation show.

"I do have a lot of holiday days accrued..." Kate began to think seriously about the prospect. Perhaps a change of scene would do her good? Somewhere in the countryside? She nodded and smiled. A real smile. The first in a long time.

THREE

Kate sat in the doctor's surgery the next evening, watching the stream of patients flitting in and out, keeping an eye on the electronic board for her name. Her usual doctor, the dour faced Dr. Malloy, had been unavailable at this short notice, so she'd taken the only appointment she could get, keen to find that elusive solution before her mini break with Rick in a fortnight. Ordinarily, she stuck with the old doctor, not because she felt he understood her situation, nor because she felt him easy to talk to, but rather because on her very first visit to discuss her anxiety, some eight years ago, Kate had ended up having an appointment with him. Not wanting to go through the whole process of discussing her symptoms with anyone else, she had ended up under his dubious care by default ever since. She certainly didn't relish the thought of discussing her mental health with someone else now, either, but needs must if she was going to be over any potential side effects of a new medication before her week away.

The sign above beeped and Kate saw that it was finally her turn. She noticed then that she had pretty much shredded the tissue in her hand. Shoving it into her pocket, she made her way slowly down the windowless corridor of closed doors, to number four. On entering, Kate was surprised to see a woman of about her own age, face welcoming and immediately putting Kate at her ease.

"What can I do for you today?" Dr. Phillips asked, silently assessing the nervous woman before her.

"I would like to change my anti-depressant," Kate began, before rushing on, not pausing to give the doctor chance to respond, "I have only been on it for five months or so, but it's not working out for me. I'm just so numb all the time."

"Okay, well there are a lot of options, let's go over your history and previous medications and see what we can do!"

Emboldened by the woman's positivity, and feeling the first shoots of hope begin to unfurl within her, Kate spoke about her history of mental illness, her panic attacks and episodes of darkness. She explained her desire to ultimately be medication-free, to be able to feel – the good and the bad events in her life – to be a true participant in her own story. The tears ran again unchecked, but Kate didn't care. The doctor was patient, not looking pointedly at her clock or appearing irritated by Kate's brain-fogged explanations.

When, at length, Kate paused and looked at her expectantly, Dr. Phillips looked up from the notes she had been making. "Okay, Kate, I think there are several things we can try. It has been proven that medication is twice as effective when used in combination with therapy and counselling. Would you be up for trying that? I can't say we'll see any noticeable difference before your time away, but hopefully the negative effects of the new medication will be easing off by then, at least. We can try a different anti-depressant, that you haven't tried before. I can make a referral to the Talk Therapy service, and I can get you access to a new app that lets you track your feelings – it's a bit like an online journal – which the therapist will also have access to and you can work on it together."

Kate was bowled over. Dr. Malloy had never offered other alternatives or options to work alongside the medication. All of Kate's CBT strategies had come from her own studies of self-help books and internet resources. When she walked out, some twenty minutes later, she felt lighter in both spirit and in mind.

"Did something happen at work today?" Sal asked, as Kate walked into their kitchen, humming to herself, "You seem… happy!"

Kate chose to ignore the shock in her best friend's tone. "I had a doctor's appointment. It went well!"

"Aw, honey, I'm so pleased!" Sal came over to embrace her. At thirty-three, and older than Kate by just two years, she had been married and divorced, and had the air of someone much older.

"Me too. I know they can't cure me. But hopefully I'll be… more like the real me before too long!" Kate felt the hope rising again and couldn't hold back the smile as she hugged her friend back.

Having met at church and gravitated towards each other as single females often do, Sal had offered Kate the spare room in her home when she'd learnt that Kate was desperate to escape her parents. Well, not desperate as such, but at twenty-eight Kate had needed to fly the nest, a stifling nest at that. Newly divorced, Sal had needed a lodger to share the bills. It had worked very well for them both.

"You must be looking forward to your time away with Patrick?" Sal pulled back and winked, causing Kate to blush.

"Yes, well, er…"

"I'm just teasing, honey, but you know I think he's right for you!"

"I know, me too, it's just… complicated."

"Love doesn't need to be complicated, you know, you can just allow yourself to feel and stop thinking once in a while!" Sal laughed as she spoke to soften the words.

Kate didn't disagree, but knowing and doing were two separate things.

FOUR

Saturday had dawned bright and crisp, almost two weeks to the day since their plan had been made. Rick had easily found a small cottage for them to rent, it being out of season, especially in wintery Scotland where they were headed. Kate tried to tamp down the butterflies in her stomach, well aware that this was a 'make or break' holiday. Not that Rick had said so explicitly, of course, but she had known his intentions that day in the coffee shop. It had been written across his face plain for all to see, he'd had enough of being kept at arm's length. After much internal debate and many discussions with Sal, Kate had decided two things. First, that she would be totally up front and honest about her mental health, something that she had skirted around, but never fully explained to her fiancé. Second, she would push through her natural barriers and give Rick some of the affection that he needed – to be honest, she craved it too, so Kate hoped that would help to bring them both closer. Decision made, she was now hovering by the window, waiting for his car to pull up outside.

"It'll be great," Sal rubbed her shoulder reassuringly, "Just relax, let him in a bit and see how you feel."

Kate knew that Sal was right, but relaxing was easier said than done where she was concerned. *I've got one last shot at this*, Kate thought morosely, *better not blow it*. Seeing the silver Nissan pull slowly round the corner, she plastered a smile to her face, pecked Sal on the cheek and grabbed her trolley case from the hallway. It was now or never.

Rick fiddled with the radio, watching as Kate emerged from the apartment building. She pulled a small case behind her, and for the first time it all seemed a bit too real, this mini break, going away together. Not for the first time, he wondered what on earth he'd been thinking to suggest it. Moved by his fiancée's emotional state in the café, Rick had acted on impulse, having had the past two weeks to repent at leisure. Not that he regretted the invitation, more that he just wasn't sure how things would work out. Was he just prolonging the inevitable? Would their love for each other be enough to fill the awkward silences and even more uncomfortable physical distance? He couldn't remember the last time they had even kissed passionately. Slapping a smile on his face, which he was sure must look as fake as Kate's own, he stepped out to help her put her case in the boot.

They were already an hour up the A1, having exhausted their usual topics of conversation – his work in the high school, her job, their parents, their flatmates. Rick fiddled with the radio again, hoping to find a comedy sketch show to fill the void.

"Would you like to stop in Edinburgh for some lunch?" he asked, taking a sideways glance at the woman next to him. She was bundled up in leggings, a huge jumper, winter boots and scarf, yet still managed to look so small. Rick couldn't help but be moved by the sight of her.

Kate hesitated, searching her mind for an excuse but coming up blank. *Now's as good a time as any, I guess,* she thought, opting for the honest answer for once. "Actually, I find big cities a bit, well, nerve wracking." She twisted the edges of her scarf between her fingers and looked across at him, waiting for a snarky reply or patronising reassurance. Yet none came.

Instead, Rick simply answered, "No worries, I know a little place just outside Berwick that you might like better? It's on a farm and they serve a lot of their own meat and ingredients in the meals. They even have a small petting zoo if you fancy stretching your legs!" Rick smiled, pleased that he'd had the forethought to look into lunch options. He hadn't fancied driving into the centre of Scotland's capital city either, and he knew from experience that Kate preferred quieter places with fewer folk.

"Thank you, yes, that sounds perfect!" Kate felt herself relax for the first time since getting in the car. She reached out and brushed the back of his hand closest to her, resting on the gear stick. It was barely anything really, just the lightest feathering of her knuckles on his skin, but Rick smiled, his blue eyes shining in the low winter sun. Perhaps this would be good for them, after all.

FIVE

As they stood in the freezing barn, their breath blowing in front of them in clouds, Rick reached to take Kate's hand in his. They had been the only visitors in the restaurant, enjoying a hearty lunch of stew and crusty bread, but here in the barn there were a few families with toddlers. All were cooing over the tiny calf, apparently born prematurely, but who was clearly a fighter. Kate's eyes had glassed over with unshed tears at the sight of it, and Rick was drawn to reach out and touch her. He'd wanted to pull her into his arms, but opted for baby steps instead.

Kate welcomed the warmth of his hand and squeezed it lightly in hers. Her new medication, whilst not having had nearly as many side effects as she'd feared, barring a bit of light-headedness and a headache for the first few days, had certainly solved the problem of feeling permanently numb. Indeed, it seemed to Kate that she had drifted to the other end of the spectrum altogether, as she was now prone to fits of weeping for no apparent reason. During a catch-up phone appointment yesterday, Dr. Phillips had reassured her that it was normal, and her body would hopefully find a balance soon, between feeling nothing and hypersensitivity. Kate tried to wipe her face surreptitiously with her free hand, instead having the opposite effect of drawing Rick's attention.

"Aw, honey," he drew her against his side then, not quite a hug, but a cuddle of sorts, and Kate accepted his offer, drawing in to him and wrapping her free arm across his coat.

"I'm okay. I'm so stupid," she sniffled, "Sorry to embarrass you!"

"Embarrass? What, in front of a few three year olds? Don't be silly!" He kissed her hair and led her away from the scene, back into the biting wind. "Let's make a move, shall we? The cottage is available from three and we've another two to three hours of driving ahead of us."

They paused at the car, as Rick fished the keys out of his pocket. Taking advantage of his distraction to hide her blushing cheeks, Kate put her arms around him properly, initiating a full hug for the first time in a long time. It felt so good, and when Rick responded by pulling her into him and seeking her lips, Kate was happy to return his kiss. It was soft and fleeting, given that their teeth were almost chattering in the cold, but it was a start, another seed of hope sewn in the garden of their relationship.

"Save the rest of that kiss for me for later!" Rick kissed her forehead as he opened the door for Kate to climb in. The warmth that filled her had as much to do with their fledgling closeness as it did the cosy car, and Kate smiled happily as they set off once more.

"Have you been to Pitten… whatsit before?" Kate asked curiously, wondering why Rick had chosen a small Scottish fishing village in the East Neuk of Fife for their break.

"Pittenweem? Once, as a child, it was a happy holiday, full of little fishing nets and hot chocolates," Rick reminisced, "It's a beautiful area, with some cute little towns and stunning beaches. It'll be just the locals at this time of year, I thought it might appeal to you."

"It does, certainly, thank you for being so thoughtful. I

can't wait to see it!" Kate had read about the cottage on its website. With views across the Firth of Forth to Edinburgh in the distance, the cottage had a cosy charm and a real wood fire to keep the frigid weather at bay. Kate couldn't wait.

As they drove across the Forth Road Bridge and onto the M90 the weather took a turn for the worse, and sleet turned to snow. Within minutes, they were driving through a blizzard, the white flakes settling on the windscreen faster than the wipers could clear them, and the visibility of the road ahead down to a few metres. Progress was achingly slow and Kate found a pop hits radio station for them to sing along to. She was adamant that nothing could shake her good mood now – though she felt the stirrings of panic begin to unfurl, she pushed it down, determined to maintain an outer composure. No panic attacks on this holiday. None.

Distracted by her own thoughts and by counting to ten to calm her panic, going to a happy place in her head… the strategies were so familiar to her… Kate did not see the red lights of the car in front of them breaking. Rick, who was looking down to the radio which had become untuned, was equally oblivious. The crunch, when it happened seconds later, despite Rick's slamming on the brakes at the last minute, seemed to slow time to a standstill. The front of their car butted into the one ahead, the screech of tyres and crunch of metal echoing around them. Yet, it was not this that was the worst of it. Behind them, a bus driver heading to Kirkcaldy had also executed an emergency stop, but the weather conditions and lack of response time, meant the inevitable happened. The bus skidded to a halt, crashing into the back of their Nissan Juke and stopping just short of crushing the couple completely. The bus's headlights were where the back seat used to be. Kate heard a keen wailing, realising in confusion that the sound came from her. More worrying, however, was Rick's silence. Unconscious, his head rested on the burst airbag, a trickle of blood running down his cheek.

"Rick! Rick, NO!" Kate's screams filled her own ears, but he did not respond. Trapped by the concertinaed car, Kate could not even get to her phone to ring for help. She had no choice but to wait for the emergency services to come. And so her praying began.

SIX

Being cut out of a car in the middle of winter is not something Kate ever wanted to repeat. The paramedics hadn't managed to bring Rick round, even for a few seconds, and they explained to a dazed Kate that the extent of his injuries couldn't be established until they got him to hospital. So, he had been released first and had gone in a haze of sirens and flashing lights, and Kate was now alone, the crunch of the saw through metal grating on her nerves and compounding her thumping headache.

"How are you holding up?" A firefighter, Doug she thought he'd said his name was, popped through the hole on Rick's side to check on her.

"Fine," Kate could think of nothing else to say. Her

mind had shut down again and only numbness remained. Matched this time by the numbness in her body. Whether from cold, shock or injury she could not tell, but for once, Kate welcomed its anaesthetic qualities.

"Won't be much longer, lassie."

The next thing Kate remembered was being in the ambulance, the reassuring tone of a paramedic talking as they took her vitals, the high-pitched siren matching the thud in her chest. She still couldn't feel her legs, but the pain relief she must've been given gave Kate a feeling of floating. Who needed legs anyway, when you could hover, just outside of yourself?

"Can I borrow that hand?" It took Kate a long moment to realise that they were referring to her hand, which was bent into a claw, clutching the small cross which hung still around her neck.

"Sorry," Kate mumbled, keen to go back to floating and not thinking. Images of the red brake lights, the snow on the windscreen, Rick's bloodied face flitted through her mind. How he hadn't made a sound as they lifted him out, the firefighters making her close her eyes so she didn't see the state of him.

"Just breathe slowly," the paramedic's words brought

Kate back to the present, to her panicked lungs, gasping for air, oblivion beckoning her once more.

The funeral took place the last week of March.

It was snowing then, too, a fitting reminder to all assembled of the accident which had taken Patrick's life. His body had been flown back to his family in Ireland, and Kate scanned them now from across the aisle as she waited for the service to start, looking for a look of recognition, some sort of reassurance, but none came. The smell of old incense and furniture polish did nothing to drown out the all-pervading sense of damp and the organ played a funeral dirge which echoed the beat of her heart. A shiver ran down Kate's back, nothing to do with the cold, and she forced down the bile from her throat. She had taken a breakfast of painkillers and coke, unable to eat much since the accident.

No-one had come to meet Kate and her parents from the airport. Her mother had commented on that none stop on the taxi drive to the hotel. How they had been left standing in the freezing cold until her dad found a taxi with wheelchair access. "How rude…" her mother had continued her tirade throughout the evening and again at breakfast, until here they sat now, Kate positioned in the space at the end of the pew, the only strangers in a sea of unfamiliar faces. Had she not needed her parents' assistance, there is no way Kate would have even considered bringing them along. Sal had offered, of course, but Kate refused to put her through it. No, it was she and she alone who deserved to suffer the stares and whispers. Her full-leg cast stretched out like a white beacon before her, a physical sign of her guilt and shame.

"Is that her then? The ice queen?" The voice was deliberately loud. Loud enough for all to hear. Its owner, a young man who now stared at her with unreserved hate, drawing the attention of all assembled.

"Well, I never!" Kate's dad was about to rise from his seat to speak on her behalf, but she put a restraining hand on his leg. Thankfully, her mother was using the bathroom and hopefully had not heard the comment. Her vocal outrage at yet another perceived affront was the last thing Kate needed right now.

"Aye, not much to look at is she? Pat should've found a good Irish girl." It was Patrick's dad who spoke now, adding to the tension in the chapel.

"Why did she even come? Hasn't she done enough?" His mother's sobbed question was the last straw.

"Get me out of here, Dad, now please," Kate could not control her tears and tried to hide her face as her father wheeled her back up the central aisle, a painfully slow process as he avoided banging her cast off the pews on either side, the condemnation in each pair of eyes following them as they went. They met her mother in the church foyer and guided her outside with them, neither wanting to explain until they were away from the scene.

"I won't get to say goodbye," Kate whispered into the icy air, her words spirited away on frozen flakes.

Now

To Catch A Feather

SEVEN

Cal paused to catch his breath, today's run in the
freezing sidewind having sucked the air out of him
and replaced it with a block of ice in his chest. He felt
in his small rucksack for the inhaler which he knew
was buried in there somewhere, seldom used, but
reassuring to have nonetheless. Today, however, he
puffed twice to open his lungs and held his breath,
taking a look at the scene around him. The cold sun
just rising on the horizon of the winter sky was offset
by the turbulent grey of the sea below. Cal had seen no
other sign of life on his morning jog along the coastal
path, save for the usual seagulls who accompanied his
route with their incessant squarks, rising and falling on
the thermal air pockets. Finally catching his breath, he
decided to walk the rest of the way into the centre of
the village, along the lane which was lined by

whitewashed cottages.

At least a quarter of the houses were holiday rentals, though there were surely no tourists here at this time of year. The first house, though, belonged to Mrs. Auchterlonie. A sturdy octogenarian, whose beady eyes missed nothing. As much as he liked the woman, Cal wasn't sure he could face a conversation with her at this early hour, knowing as he did that she would be in his coffee shop at eleven on the dot for her usual pot of tea and currant bun. Feeling slightly guilty at his evasive tactics, Cal mustered up the breath for one last sprint around the corner, aiming to get halfway along the little lane before he began walking, thus avoiding any unwanted chat. It seemed like a great plan, until the wind, stronger now that he was on this side of the path, threw Cal's floppy hair in front of his eyes, causing him to stumble mid-run. Blinded by both his fringe and the grit that was whipped up from the rocky shore below, Cal reached awkwardly to the side, trying to balance himself on the nearest house.

"Excuse me!" The indignant remark caught Cal off guard and he realised, shocked, that his hand was touching smooth material rather than cold stone. Jumping back stunned, he brushed his hair out of his face long enough to see the annoyed features of a woman staring back at him. Huddled against the wall of the cottage, sitting on a fold-out fisherman's chair, she had an easel in front of her which was held in place by two well-positioned sandbags. Wrapped in a thick winter coat with a hat pulled almost to her eyes, Cal saw the few red ringlets which ran in tendrils down her face. Shocked, he realised too late that he had been staring. He was unused to seeing new people here at this time of year, especially beautiful women. And what on earth was she doing out at this time of day with the sun barely risen in the sky?

"I'm so sorry!" he tried to apologise, but the words died on his lips, when the woman simply raised an unimpressed eyebrow and turned back to her painting. Considering himself dismissed, Cal set off at a run again, keen to get away from the scene of his embarrassment. Reaching the end of the row of houses, and seeing his own café and flat above just along the harbour, Cal chanced a quick peek backwards. As much to reassure himself that he hadn't imagined her as anything else. She was indeed real, and Cal was startled to see that the woman was looking back in his direction too. The distance was too far and the weather too wild for him to see her face clearly, but he could feel her eyes on him, and Cal wasn't sure whether to feel warmed or worried by the connection.

Pushing the stranger out of his mind, he rushed home,

keen to reach a hot shower and a strong coffee. Josh would be ready for school, and Cal liked to send him on his way with dinner money and a bacon buttie before heading straight into the coffee shop to catch the few earlybirds who liked a takeaway hot drink on the way to work.

"Dad! Get a shufty on, will ya! Ave gotta get goin' to meet Evan!" Cal smiled as he took his trainers off. His son was a bigger nag than any fisherman's wife.

"Alright, keep your hair on!" He ruffled his son's hair, as the lad tried to duck away and went straight into the small kitchen to set the bacon frying. His shower would have to wait.

EIGHT

Kate absentmindedly rubbed her shoulder where the stranger has touched her. It didn't hurt, he had barely made contact, but she was so startled by the connection she'd felt when she looked in his eyes that Kate couldn't get the image of his face out of her head. Not that he'd been particularly attractive, with his bright red cheeks and sweat-soaked brow, but Kate has seen kindness in his brown eyes that had warmed her, if only for a second.

Dragging her attention back to her painting, she decided enough was enough for now. The scene before her, the beautiful Firth of Forth stretching out from a thin beach of wet sand and smooth, flat rock, was stunning in its stormy winter greys, but Kate was not feeling it today. As always, her mind was focussed on her next dose of painkillers. Not that she really needed them anymore – not for pain anyway. Her leg throbbed occasionally, especially when she walked too long and too far, but it was mostly for herself that she took the drugs now. To feed the addiction that had sprung up when she was at her lowest and unaware of the dangers.

She had been in the village for three days now, and had not ventured from the cottage. Kate had come here to find refuge, and so far the small village of Pittenweem had afforded her that. What had possessed her to take her three month sabbatical in the very place which reminded her most of the accident? Kate wasn't sure. Perhaps it was just another chapter in the book of punishments which she had doled out to herself. It had seemed fitting, that on this the fifth anniversary of Patrick's death, she should come to the place they had intended to visit together. To see it for the first time. Even managing to book into the same cottage which had been their destination on that fateful day. Now she was here, however, Kate wondered how she would cope with the guilt and grief which washed over her and sucked her down below its surface. It was no longer grief for Rick, she knew, her therapist had explained as much several times. Rather it was grief for herself. For the Kate who had also died that day. And that knowledge added to her guilt. Guilt upon guilt, until she could barely breathe.

Yesterday, and the day before that, Kate had spent the morning in bed, hiding under the covers to try to avoid feeling. It hadn't worked. She had cried until her throat was raw and her head pounded, but still sleep would not come. Not without the sleeping tablets – another dirty secret. Today, she was determined to do something else. Walk the short distance into the village, perhaps, to the little coffee shop she had seen advertised on the Pittenweem Tourist Information web page. *Yes*, she thought to herself, *I can manage that at least.* A small art supplies shop had also been featured on the web page, three doors down from the café, and that had certainly attracted her interest. Art was a new hobby – well, new since the accident anyway, something Sal and her parents thought might take her mind off things, or at least give her an outlet to express herself. It had worked, to a degree, and now Kate spent her weekends in the wilds of Northumberland, sitting silently in bird hides or on the top of grassy slopes keen to get the best view. It gave her a reason to avoid company, more than anything, to refuse invitations to socialise, though those were few and far between nowadays.

Wrapping her scarf twice around her neck to ward off the icy blast as she opened the front door, Kate caught sight of the clock in the hallway. Five to eleven. How a shower and putting away her paints had taken that long, Kate had no idea. Everything seemed to take her an age nowadays, as she had neither energy nor enthusiasm for any task. *Never mind*, she thought resignedly, *I'm on my way now.*

"Good morning, Dearie!" The croaky voice startled Kate and she turned slowly on the doorstep. "I thought I'd seen someone arriving the other day!" The woman must be eighty if she was a day, Kate thought, as she watched the hunched figure hurry to join her. They almost had matching walking sticks – *How charming,* Kate thought sardonically, wondering if she could make an excuse to duck inside again. No such luck. The older woman had already linked her free arm though Kate's and was propelling them both up the small street.

"Hello," it was all Kate could manage. She had no intention of conversing.

"Well, it's fair blowing a hoolie the day!" the woman carried on unperturbed, "Strange time of year to be coming for a holiday!" She cast a long sideways glance in Kate's direction, clearly waiting on an explanation, but tut tutted when none was forthcoming and ploughed on. "Anyway, Cameron will have a warm welcome for us! He knows I like my elevenses prompt!"

I'm sure he does, Kate thought, but held her tongue.

Between their mutual limping and the strong southerly wind, it took what seemed like a very long five minutes to reach the brightly painted door of the small coffee shop. They almost fell in on a gust of wind, Kate having to grab the end of the counter to steady herself.

"Good day to you, laddie!" the older woman rushed ahead, unlinking from Kate and leaving her apparently stranded in the doorway.

"Good morning Mrs. Auchterlonie... and guest!" Cal quirked a surprised eyebrow at the woman who clutched his counter, catching her breath and steadying herself. The woman from this morning. He could feel the blush rising from his polo neck jumper right up his cheeks and across the bridge of his nose. "I have your usual table in the window, of course," on autopilot, he escorted his usual customer to her favourite table.

Kate paused, unsure whether to just ask for a coffee to go. Too late, she realised she was being spoken to.

"Aye, now don't be shy lassie! Get yourself across here and give me some company! It's not often that an old woman like me gets to have a good natter!"

Resigned, Kate made her way slowly to the table, her cane beating her approach on the wooden floor. She studiously avoided the eyes of the man, whom she just now recognised as the runner from this morning, and angled herself into the tight corner seat as gracefully as she could manage. One quick cuppa and she was out of here.

NINE

"Constance Auchterlonie, pleased to meet you!" A small, weathered hand was outstretched towards Kate and she shook it gently before placing her own quickly back in her lap, lest her companion saw the tremor that had been a permanent feature since the accident. Doctors had found no physical explanation, other than anxiety and potential post-traumatic stress disorder. It was another shameful secret. "And you are?"

Kate realised she had zoned out again. "Ah, Katherine, Kate Winters."

"A pretty name, Katherine, I once knew a girl of that name, back before I was wed, when I worked in the fishmarket, a bonnie lassie she were…"

And so it began.

Mrs. Auchterlonie's order arrived as if by magic and the man stood at the table looking slightly flustered until the woman finished her latest anecdote.

"And so they eloped… can you imagine that! With a wee babby on the way to boot!" Constance paused for a breath, looking rather irritated at the interruption. "Thank you Cameron. Ah, have you met Miss Winters?"

"I have not had that pleasure," Cal directed a small rueful smile in Kate's direction. "Cameron McAllister, Cal," He nodded by way of greeting and Kate was grateful that he did not expect her to shake hands.

"Kate," She whispered, making eye contact only briefly. He had scrubbed up well, to be sure, and Kate tried not to smell his fresh scent or stare at his neat stubble.

"What can I get you, Kate?"

For a moment, she'd forgotten why she was there entirely. Never mind, she had Mrs. Auchterlonie to recite the question for her, as if speaking to a child.

"He's asking if you want a drink, dear!"

"Yes, thanks I'll have, ah a cappuccino."

"Coming right up!" The poor man seemed relieved to get away back behind his counter, and Kate couldn't blame him. The conversation at the table – if it could be called that since it was completely one sided, a monologue, perhaps? – continued at pace, moving on from the heady 1960s of the woman's twenties and into the '70s when she was married with children. It was amazing the scandals she could remember, the family histories… Kate had to admit that she was grateful to not have to speak about herself, and settled into her chair, letting the woman's words drift over and around her, their Scottish lilt almost melodic.

"So," Constance peered over the top of her thick-rimmed glasses, "What brings you to our little village, Miss. Winters? Winters in Winter, ha!" She giggled at her own joke and her humour was almost infectious, though not quite enough to quash the terror that rose in Kate at the thought that she was now required to explain herself. The familiar feeling of panic and suffocation began and she clawed at her scarf, still around her neck though her coat had been shrugged off a while ago. Finally managing to loosen the offensive item, Kate took a few deep breaths before replying. The astute eyes of the woman opposite never left her face.

"Well, I'm taking a sabbatical, an extended leave from

my job, and I thought I'd spend my three months here, painting your beautiful landscape."

"Oh, I knew a painter once, very affable man he was. Batted for the other team, of course…" and she was off again, giving Kate a chance to regroup and calm her beating heart. Looking up, Kate saw that Cameron was studying her as he cleaned the coffee machine. Caught looking, he quickly returned his attention to his work, leaving Kate with an unsettling feeling, something she had not felt for a very long time – attraction.

"So, we can make this our daily thing, since you're going to be a regular in the village for the springtime?" Constance Auchterlonie looked hopefully at Kate, and she didn't have the heart to refuse.

"Well, I, er, maybe not every day, Mrs. Auchterlonie. Perhaps, um twice a week?" Kate tried to push a compromise, but the older woman was having none of it.

"Hmm, we'll see. We can start tomorrow and take it from there! You can walk me home now!"

Having twisted and turned to get into her coat, Kate struggled to get out of her chair, feeling ineffectually behind her for her walking stick which should have been propped against the wall where she had left it. Yet all she could feel were the rough-hewn surfaces of bare bricks. A small cough brought her back to the present.

Cal stood, one arm hooked in Mrs. Auchterlonie's elbow and the other brandishing the stick. "Oh, er thanks," Kate felt her cheeks heat at the knowledge that he knew she had a disability. That she wasn't functioning correctly. *Of course he knows!* She chastised herself, *he saw you walk in with it!* And yet the sight of the man standing there holding her walking aid somehow made the knowledge of it more real, and Kate grabbed the stick back from him, undoubtedly rudely, before grinding out, "Lead the way, then!"

Both the man and the old woman looked at her with calculating eyes – warm eyes, to be fair, but certainly assessing her. Or was that just in her mind? Her paranoia coming to the fore once more? Kate couldn't tell. All she wanted was to escape back to the little cottage on the sea front and hide herself away from their scrutiny. From everyone's scrutiny in fact.

The wind had an added companion now – drizzle. The kind of sideways, slanted drenching that soaks through to your bones and leaves you feeling frozen to your core. As they opened the door to the jingling of the bell above, the weather hit them like a solid wall, and Kate had to push into it, struggling with her stick in one hand and Mrs. Auchterlonie in the other. The older woman, however, was a hardy sort and simply tied her rain hood under her chin in a bow and braced herself for the walk, shouting her goodbyes to Cal as they began making their slow way along the front street, known as Mid Shore. Walking past her own door, Kate guided the old woman to her house, some five doors further down, refusing the offer of more tea and a light lunch.

"I'll be seeing you on the morrow then lassie," the kindly woman patted Kate's shoulder before disappearing inside, leaving the younger woman staring after her in the wet, wondering how on earth she'd managed to get herself a daily coffee companion when she'd come with the intention of living as much of a reclusive life as possible.

Trudging the few steps back to her own doorway, fishing around in her pocket for the large key, the image of the man from the coffee shop came unbidden to mind. Cal. Kate blinked rapidly – as much to clear her head as to remove the water droplets from her lashes. The time for attraction was long gone. With Patrick in fact. She was older now, broken, and she neither wanted nor needed a man, just as none would ever want her broken form again.

TEN

Cal busied himself cleaning the counter for the umpteenth time that morning. Other than his regulars, the day was going slowly. Well, since Kate Winters had left anyway. He had been shocked to see her there, in his space, the same woman he had inadvertently leaned against that morning, and with none other than Constance Auchterlonie.

At first, he'd thought maybe they were related, and Kate was staying with the old woman, but he'd quickly come to realise that Kate was simply caught up in Constance's energy, the way many newcomers unwittingly were. She liked to take them under her wing, especially when she sensed a lost soul. They were her passion and her purpose. If Cal had a pound for every time he'd heard her say "I am the Lord's servant, laddie, he sends me the lost sheep and I bring them back to the flock!" he'd be a rich man today.

Hadn't he himself been one of her 'lost sheep' just a few years before? He was under no illusion that the daily visits, which had started right after Sally died, weren't more for his benefit than Constance's. Whilst she enjoyed a good cuppa and a natter, he knew that she came in every day, regular as clockwork, to check on him and Josh. The woman had certainly seen her own fair share of heartache, and Cal knew that her hardened exterior hid a very soft centre. She had adopted him and Josh as her own, bringing them pies and soups, feeding them up as the grief ravaged their minds and bodies. And when he'd finally emerged on the other side, broken but not defeated, she had been there to support him and Josh in any way she could. A true treasure.

And then there was Kate. She had seen her fair share of trauma too, he was sure. From the haunted look in her eyes, to the closed-off demeanour and, of course, her obvious physical difficulties, Cal could recognise the signs of someone still in the throes of their grief. She had affected him. More than he'd like to admit, to be honest. Not just her looks, though of course she was more than just attractive. With her red curls and green eyes she could be on the cover of any Scottish tale from times gone by. No, it was something in her which attracted him – the recognition of a kindred spirit, perhaps? But what would he do with this realisation? Nothing. Not a single thing, Cal knew, as he had sworn off women after Sally. The love of his life, he had been devastated when the cancer took her and promised himself that no other woman could ever compare to his childhood sweetheart. Besides, he had Josh, only nine at the time, who was his top priority.

Nevertheless, Cal's mind strayed to Kate far more than it should have during the day, and he began to consider another freezing run after closing time just to distract himself. *One new face in the village and I'm acting like a lovesick schoolboy!* He remonstrated with himself, ineffectually trying to deny the attraction he felt. They just didn't get many visitors at this time of year, that was all it was. Especially not auburn haired beauties who looked like they could do with a big cuddle. *Arrgghh. Enough!*

Kate built up the log fire and settled down under a blanket on the sofa to read her book. The wind rattled the old windows and a draft came in under the door, but the place was homely and she felt safe here. One tiny sitting room, a postcard sized kitchen, a narrow staircase, bedroom and bathroom were all the house offered, yet Kate had felt at home as soon as she'd entered the place. Patrick had made a good choice! When had she stopped calling him Rick, she wondered, suddenly, the thought having never crossed her mind before. She scanned her memories and realised it was after the funeral, when she'd known for sure that she didn't have the right to call him by a shortened, familiar name. His family were right, it had been her fault. He wouldn't have even been on that stretch of road if he wasn't trying to rescue their relationship. She should've let him end it that day in the coffee shop. Poor, poor man. His beautiful life extinguished, by her.

Kate reached up to where her cross used to hang, out of pure habit. It hadn't rested against her collar bone for years now. Discarded, along with her bibles and study guides, and all relics of her former life. The necklace had been replace by a string of raw amethyst chunks, which the spiritual healer had assured Kate would give her peace and calm. It had been years, and Kate still couldn't speak for the truth in that, yet she continued to wear the item for what it symbolised more than anything. The new her. No longer restricted by the confines of religion or organised beliefs, she had tried to find her own path. To unravel the truths of the universe. *And how's that working out for you?*

Realising that she was crying, Kate scrubbed the tears from her face and stood up on unsteady feet to reach her bag of painkillers from the coffee table. *Time for a little bit of oblivion,* she decided, not caring that this break was meant to be a time to wean off her addiction. Recovery could begin tomorrow, today she needed a release – a reprieve from the thoughts that haunted her day and night, and which only the strongest drugs could now provide, she having become too acclimatised to the weaker versions. Downing three pills with a swig of cold coffee, Kate snuggled further under the blanket and let herself drift off to a place with no ghosts – where neither Patrick nor young Kate could reach her.

ELEVEN

The hammering on the door finally brought Kate back to her senses. She had no idea how long it had been going on, having thought at first that it was the pounding in her head that she could hear. She glanced at the old clock on the mantle – five past eleven. Even that small movement caused a dizziness such that her senses where whirling and Kate thought she might vomit. Why would someone be hammering on her door this late in the evening? Her panic began to rise, the familiar feeling adding to her distress. Then she spotted that her curtains were still open and a grey sunlight shone though. Oh God, how many pills had she taken? The fire had long since died out, but it wasn't the cold which sent a shiver down Kate's spine. The packets lay out on the floor beneath her. How many tablets had there been originally? She remembered taking three Tramadol in the afternoon, then had a hazy recollection of more tablets and some Oramorph throughout the evening. And still that thudding would not cease. "I'm coming," she tried to shout, but it was merely a scratchy croak. Kate struggled to pull her senses together and get her fogged mind in order, but to no avail. She couldn't bring herself to get off the couch, each limb feeling like stone, nor could she keep her head upright, preferring to let it sink back down onto the cushion.

Constance gave up her rapping on the front door and decided to peer in the front window instead. At first she saw nothing in the gloom of the room, but just when she was about to go back to her hammering, a small movement from the sofa opposite the fire caught her eye. And then she saw it, the cascade of red curls hanging down almost to the floor, their owner lying prostate on the settee. Constance muffled a shriek of concern and took off as fast as her arthritic legs and walking stick could carry her, to the post office where she knew Miss. Dodds kept a spare set of keys for the owners, in case of emergency. Only a few steps down the path, however she was met with a sprinting Cameron, hurrying up to meet her, his face a picture of worry.

"Connie! When you were late I started to become

concerned! I've shut the shop to come and find you!"

"Tis not me you need to worry about, laddie! Quick run to the postal office and get the keys for the Spencers' place."

"This one, why?" Cameron took a turn at the window where Constance had returned to squint through the glass, shocked when he saw the still figure of Kate slumped on the furniture. "I'll be right back. Keep knocking to try to rouse her!" He set off at pace, the way he had just come, into the centre of the village.

Returning less than ten minutes later, the sweat dripping from his forehead, Cal brandished the key and unlocked the door to Kate's property. Constance rushed past him as he bent to catch his breath and straight into the living room, where Kate had fallen back into a deathlike slumber.

"Lassie! Wake up now!" the older woman shook Kate's shoulders gently until eventually her face twitched and one eye opened. "That's it, come back to us now!"

Joining her, Cal stooped to pick up the packets from the floor. He recognised them immediately, as his Sally had been the owner of such a wide range of tablets by the time she passed, it was like they had their own pharmacy.

"I'll call an ambulance," he stated matter of factly.

Hearing the one word, as if through a tunnel, Kate managed to speak. "No! No ambulance! No need!" She had not set foot in a hospital since the accident, and even in her befuddled state, her brain registered her panic at the thought of it.

"Okay, let's stay calm," Constance reassured, whilst directing a sharp shake of the head at Cal, who stood wringing his hands, feeling helpless. A feeling which was far too familiar to be comfortable. "Aye, we'll get you sat up and a glass of water followed by a cup of sweet tea and we can go from there." The woman took charge, bustling to the small kitchen whilst Cal gently helped Kate to a sitting position, propping some cushions behind her back to keep her upright.

"You'll be okay," he whispered, more to himself than to his patient, "I've got you. Lean on me." He sat down beside Kate, gently angling her so that her head rested on his shoulder.

"Thanks," Kate whispered, grateful for the firm body next to her and the comfort and warmth he offered. Her own body had now begun to shake uncontrollably, and before she could stop it a huge sob broke out from her mouth. She shocked herself with the noise of it, and Cal immediately turned slightly so that he could draw her closer to him.

"Och now, you'll be right," he stroked her hair and whispered against her forehead. "I know you feel scared, but I'm here. And Constance of course. We'll have ye right in no time." The words flowed as easily as they always had, Cal having said them all too often in the past. He reached out and took the shaking hand closest to him, nestling it firmly in his own, larger palm and trying to channel some comfort through the tiny connection.

Kate felt too unwell to be self-conscious at how vulnerable she was being. Her head throbbed and the crying had a will of its own, bursting out of her with the force of years' worth of pent-up emotions.

"Let it out, there," Cal rubbed her shoulder and thanked Constance as she passed him a quilt from the bed to wrap around Kate's fragile, weeping frame. He helped her to take small sips from a cup of water, before Constance reappeared with three large mugs on a tray.

"Ah see you've got no choccie bikkies in there!" Constance said, trying to lighten the mood. "What woman doesn't have a secret stash?" She winked and Kate forced a weak smile as she accepted Cal's help to lift her mug to her mouth. Her whole body felt as if she was floating. She knew that by tomorrow she would be absolutely mortified at the memory of this, but for now Kate accepted the help that was offered. She had to admit, albeit begrudgingly, that it was nice to be taken care of for once. She had let no one close since the accident, even moving out of Sal's to a tiny bedsit on her own. *And look where that's got me!* she thought ruefully.

TWELVE

Kate couldn't make out the hushed conversation that was going on in the kitchen, but she knew that they were discussing her. Who else? She was the only one causing a scene. Struggling to her feet, Kate tried to walk to the other room to join them, just as Cal emerged through the door. Good thing too, as she took one step then lurched forwards and into his arms.

"Steady there, you shouldn't have tried to get up!" he scolded her gently, accepting her head which Kate had no choice but to rest on his chest, so dizzy was she. He pulled her close to support her more firmly, and stroked the back of Kate's head as the sobs returned full force.

"Och, why are you standing, lassie?" Constance had joined them and fussed around like a mother hen, directing Cal as he helped Kate back to the settee and then tucking the quilt around her as if she were a poorly child.

"I'm okay. Thank you, you can both get about your day," Kate whispered.

Sitting down beside her, her hips creaking at the movement, the older woman took Kate's hand gently. "Now, listen to me. I know you don't want to be visiting the hospital. And I don't blame you. I had enough of that place myself when my Billy was on his way out. God rest his soul. No, now you're conscious again, we'll try to avoid that. But you must realise lassie that you can't be left alone until all that stuff's out of yer system, and until I'm happy you won't be pulling anything like that again!"

It was like having a very firm, very kind grandmother – something Kate had never experienced, her own grandparents having lived down South and passing away before she was old enough to remember the annual visits to see them. "Oh no, that's not nec…" Contradicting Constance was, apparently, futile. The older woman made a 'tsshh' sound between her teeth and carried on talking as if Kate had not spoken.

"So, I will stay here with you for the day," she paused as if a thought had just occurred to her then, casting a sly glance at Cal who stood silently opposite them, she continued, "And then you will go to spend the night at Cal's so that he can help you if you have need."

"No!" Both Kate and Cal spoke in unison. Clearly, this was not what had been agreed upon in the kitchen!

"Yes now, tis the best solution all round. I'm an old lady, I can't be getting up to check on people in the night now, can I?" The small smirk told Cal that she knew she'd won.

"That's low, Connie, pulling the old lady card," he muttered, "we all know you're as strong as an ox!"

"You keep your ox insults to yerself, cheeky!" But he could tell she was happy with the arrangement. Cal had a sinking feeling that the woman who had been like a grandmother to him was now trying to meddle in his love life. His non-existent love life. Well, he was having none of it, but that was a conversation for later. Right now he needed to get back to the shop for the last of any lunchtime trade.

"Well, I'll be heading off then ladies. Kate, I'll be back to collect you at around six."

"No really, there's no…" but he had already left the room, and Kate was left with Constance, who was already turning on the TV for her daily dose of Bargain Hunt. Laying her head back, Kate let her eyes drift shut again.

The day was already drawing to a close when Kate awoke. The streetlights shone through the small window, and Constance was tapping her lightly on the shoulder. "Here, lassie, have this soup now, to warm you before you go to Cameron's. He's a good lad that one, but not much of a cook if you know what I mean!"

Kate allowed herself to be spoon fed, before testing her legs once more. She was desperate for the toilet and didn't want the older woman to have to support her to the bathroom. Thankfully, the extra sleep had let more of the drugs work their way through her system and Kate felt stronger and less dizzy. Still weak, but at least more independent. Task complete, she staggered to the bedroom and packed a small bag. *One night. One night to keep Constance happy and that is it.* She added her sketch pad and pencils to the pile, deciding that if she had an occupation there would be no need for awkward conversation with her host.

More hushed whispers, this time from the hallway,

alerted Kate to Cameron's arrival. Taking the stairs two at a time, he rushed straight into her bedroom without knocking.

"You should've waited! I could have helped you up the stairs!" His words seemed angry but his face showed nothing but pure concern. Kate knew that he spoke from a place of care for her, and so bit her tongue on the quick retort that sprang up.

"Wait here while I see Connie home and I'll be right back," Cal held Kate's elbow as she lowered to the sofa, having exhausted herself with only those small tasks and getting back down the stairs. Not finding the energy to protest, she did as instructed after thanking the older woman for her help. Regret and depression were now settling over her like a blanket. Kate welcomed it reluctantly. Old acquaintances, she knew that the feelings would intensify now that the drugs had worn off. She needed to be alone, it was just a shame that Cameron McAllister had other ideas.

THIRTEEN

Cal still couldn't quite get his head around the day he'd had. From finding Kate passed out and all the emotions and memories that had brought to the surface, to being cornered into inviting her to stay the night, and having to explain to Josh why they had a female guest… it was almost too much to get his tired head around. Of course, he hadn't told the lad about the painkillers, just that Kate was new to the village and feeling unwell. He fully intended to take her to the local health centre in Anstruther the next morning, come hell or high water and have her checked out, though he suspected that her illness was more one of heart and spirit than of body.

"Thank you," Kate gratefully accepted the coffee he

offered. She'd drunk enough weak tea that day to sink a ship, and craved the caffeine kick Cal's freshly-ground beans provided.

"It's no bother," he replied, awkward now that they were alone together. Josh was playing video games in his room, and the silence stretched out between the pair uncomfortably. He watched as Kate scribbled away on her sketch pad. Moving to sit in the chair next to her at the small table to get a better look, Cal was startled by the outline of a kestrel. She certainly had talent.

"Did you do that from memory?" he asked, not seeing a book anywhere around.

"I did. I spend a lot of time in the countryside when I'm not at work."

"It's fantastic!"

"Thank you," Kate blushed under his scrutiny, unused to showing her work to anyone. Her dizziness had receded in the past hour and she just had the fatigue and headache to contend with.

"What do you do, in your day job I mean?" Cameron was genuinely interested in the woman sat next to him, and hoped to persuade her to lower her guard slightly.

"I'm a veterinary nurse. Small animals – pets mostly."

Cal smiled and watched as Kate deliberately smudged some of her pencil marks, giving the feathers extra depth and realism. Finally looking up, she realised she would be rude not to make some conversation with the man who was trying so hard to engage her.

"Have you always lived in the village, or in Fife?" she asked, laying her pencil back in the tin and snapping it shut.

"Ah, no, no, I'm from Elgin actually. Up North."

"I've never been north of Perth. I've heard the highlands are very beautiful. What tempted you down here… though Pittenweem is also stunning of course!" Kate stumbled over the words, unused to just chatting with anyone.

"Well, I met my wife at Aberdeen university, but she came from Fife, so after we graduated we moved back here to be close to her mam, who was alone."

"Your wife?" Kate left the question hanging in the air, like an arrow with no direction it seemed to draw both of their attention. She regretted it instantly.

"My late wife, Sally." Cal got up to take the coffee cups to the sink, annoyed with himself. He had started the conversation, yet it was he who was now running away from it. Living in a village where everyone knew the other's business, it had been a long time since he'd had to explain about Sally to anyone.

Coming back to his chair after taking a moment to regroup, Cameron said, "She died three years ago. Cancer." He turned his mouth in distaste as if the word itself were poison.

"I'm so sorry," Kate reached out to touch his hand lightly, then pulled back just as quickly, not knowing where the gesture had come from.

"And you?" Cal asked, sensing an opening into the truth behind the woman's visit, "do you have relatives here? What made you choose our village?"

"Well, I, I nearly visited five years ago, but there was," Kate paused, unsure how much she wanted to reveal. She twisted her hands together in her lap – the tremor in her hand was more noticeable since yesterday and even more so now as she became anxious at the direction the conversation was taking. "There was an accident." She turned away to fiddle with her sketchbook, making clear there would be no more information forthcoming.

"I'm sorry to hear that," Cal said, his voice low and

gentle. His heart hammering in his chest at her admission. Wanting to ask more, he checked himself and instead enquired, "and you'll be with us for...?"

"Three months," Kate looked into his eyes for the first time that evening, not comfortable with making eye contact generally. She saw the kindness, the empathy there and felt herself relax slightly, "until the end of May."

"Och, the springtime is beautiful here, not as bonnie as the summer mind you, but you're in for a treat! Plenty to draw and paint. I can take you to some of the sights, if you like?" *Where did that offer come from?* Cal watched as Kate's eyes rounded in surprise, matching his own, no doubt! It wasn't like he didn't have enough to do without playing tour guide!

"Really?" Kate wasn't sure what to say. To have a companion on a few visits would certainly be helpful. She mulled it over for a moment.

"Of course, it would be my pleasure." Cal wiped the bead of sweat that had formed on his forehead. How was it so hot in here all of a sudden?

"In that case, let me do a few hours in the coffee shop in return, clearing tables for you."

"That's not necessary, what with your…" Cal looked briefly at her stick resting against the wall and immediately regretted it. The words hadn't come out in the courteous way he'd intended, even he could hear how they sounded.

"I'm not an invalid!" Kate pushed her chair back and the screeching sound filled the deafening silence.

"I'm so sorry," Cal jumped to his feet, grabbing her elbow to keep her there a moment longer while he explained himself. When Kate flinched at the contact, he pulled his hand back as if burned. "I only meant that I made the offer without any strings attached." He sat down heavily and ran his hands through his hair.

"I know exactly what you meant," Kate replied harshly and, grabbing her stick, made her way to the bedroom she'd been shown at the back of the apartment.

FOURTEEN

The moment the door was closed behind her, Kate sank down onto the bed and the floodgates opened. She let the tears flow unhindered down her face, until her vision was blurred and her nose streaming. It was at this perfect moment that Cal chose to knock on the door. *Damn!* Kate muttered, dragging her hand across her face roughly. It was the man's own house, she couldn't very well refuse him entry. Glancing around quickly, it was then that realisation hit – this was Cameron's bedroom. *Oh no!*

"Come in!" Kate knew she couldn't hide the truth of her upset, since it was plastered all over her wet face.

Cal entered the room cautiously, peering round the

door first to make sure his guest was fully dressed. He thought he'd heard her say it was safe to come in, but it was so faint he couldn't be sure. The moment he set his eyes on her, Cal rushed to the bed, kneeling in front of Kate though not touching her.

"Oh sweetheart," he tried to think of anything helpful to say, as he attempted to drag his gaze from her watery green eyes, "Do you need a hug?"

Kate thought a moment, but knew she'd be lying if she said no, and they both deserved better than that right now. She simply nodded and leaned forward to rest her forehead on Cal's shoulder. He shuffled forward and put his arms around her back, gently pulling her closer into his embrace.

"You've had a difficult twenty-four hours," he whispered, "your emotions are probably all over the place," he paused, unsure whether to ask the question which had been on his lips all day. He decided to just say it. "Those pills, Kate, you didn't mean to…?"

"What?" Kate lifted her head quickly, her face now just inches from his. "No! No, I didn't! I just need them to… to… relax!"

"Okay sweetheart, I just needed to know whether I should be checking on you during the night…" his arms remained around her and he could feel her breath on his face. Cal cleared his throat, which was suddenly very dry.

Kate knew she should pull away, that this was definitely too close for comfort, especially since she barely knew the man in whose arms she rested. Yet, she felt she had known him a whole lot longer. It was strange, this kind of unspoken understanding which they shared. Briefly analysing her feelings whilst not taking her eyes off his face, Kate was surprised when she didn't feel awkward or embarrassed. The moment lengthened. Brown eyes staring into green, their lips almost touching.

"Dad! Where's my PE top for tomorrow?" Cal wasn't sure whether he should be disappointed or thankful for his son's shouted intrusion. Certainly, nothing could happen between him and his guest, so it was perhaps just as well he'd been brought back to his senses.

"I'll be right there, mate!" Cal replied, pulling back slowly so that Kate didn't lose her balance on the edge of the bed. To her, he whispered, "I'll pop back in shortly to grab some things."

"I don't want to take your bed, Cameron, I can sleep on the sofa!"

"Don't be daft! Josh's got bunk beds so I'll just camp in with him!"

Kate nodded her head as he retreated from the room. She could only imagine how she looked with her swollen eyes and blotchy face, her hair still a tangle from last night. When had she started being bothered about how she looked anyway? When had she become so needy? Not wanting to think about it right now, she took the opportunity to quickly use the small, shared bathroom and to pull on her pyjamas. Her skin and hair would have to wait for some attention until the morning, as the tiredness was so intense now, nothing but bed beckoned.

When Cal knocked gently and poked his head around the bedroom door some twenty minutes later, he found Kate curled up on her side, fast asleep on his bed. He tiptoed up to her and reached for the tartan wool blanket which lay across the foot of the bed, pulling it over without disturbing her. He knew he'd be lying if he told himself that he wasn't attracted to the beautiful woman sleeping so soundly. But he wasn't in the market for a partner. He had Josh, just about to become a teenager, and needing him more than ever. No, he was a dad first and foremost. Besides, there wasn't much call in the dating market for forty-two year old single dads anyway. And Kate? Well, that lovely lady seemed to have her own ghosts to deal with.

Grabbing his own nightwear and clothes for the morning, Cameron snook out of the room again, closing the door softly behind him. Going to tidy the kitchen before bed, he spotted Kate's sketch pad on the table where she'd left it after her quick exit earlier. He tried so hard to resist the urge to have a flick through, at the secrets it held, but evidently not hard enough. Before he'd even fully registered his actions, the thick notebook was in his hands. Cal sank down onto the nearest chair and lay the book out on the table once more, this time with it open on the first page. He knew it was a bad idea. He knew it was an invasion of privacy. But somehow he couldn't stop himself.

A range of random flowers and birds adorned the first few pages, dotted haphazardly around the white sheets. In fact, Cal was almost going to close the pad and leave well alone, when the sixth page revealed something completely different. A car, its back half crumpled almost beyond recognition, a bus wedged into its behind. The picture was smudged with fingerprints, as if it had been looked at and touched many times. It almost reached out and grabbed Cal, so stark was the scene. Turning the page, his heart beating fast in his chest, Cal found something even worse. A man, only his profile in view, squashed behind an air bag, and a shattered windscreen, blood dripping down his forehead. That was shocking in itself, but nothing compared to the woman who stood to the side watching him. Clearly Kate, she stood upright, but held her hands to her chest which had been rent open. In her clutched palms, her own heart sat, dripping blood onto the white snow below.

Cal slammed the book shut and lowered his face into his hands. He wasn't altogether sure what he'd just seen, but one thing was certain, the poor woman in the room next to him had been to Hell and back, much the same as he himself had. It brought back feelings Cal had hoped were safely buried, and he allowed himself a moment to feel their ferocity – the loss, the anger, the helplessness, the loneliness – until he eventually dragged himself off to Josh's room where he knew sleep would be slow to come.

FIFTEEN

Kate awoke before sunrise, her headache gone but her mouth and throat parched. What was more, her body craved the painkillers which she'd normally have had during the night. Tiptoeing silently from the room, she turned the corner to the kitchen only to bump into something firm but soft. The sinking feeling in her gut and the fresh, woodsy smell, told her what she knew without looking up – Cameron.

"I'm so sorry," she mumbled, "Just need a glass of water and my sketch book."

"Not a problem," Cal looked down at the woman who was shuffling back a few paces to let him past. Her red curls framing her face in wild disarray, the Care Bears pyjamas that looked like they'd seen better days. He couldn't help the small smile that graced his lips. "Can I get you something to eat, a bacon sandwich maybe?"

"No, thank you, I'm…" the words died on her lips as Kate's stomach let out a traitorous growl of protest.

"I'll take that as a yes then!" Cal turned back into the kitchen, chuckling to himself.

Kare could feel her cheeks heating and she shuffled behind him like a child. The thought piqued her somewhat, and after briefly analysing it as she sat down on one of the stools at the small breakfast bar, Kate was niggled to realise that she didn't want Cameron, or anyone, thinking of her as a child. Or treating her as one. She was a grown woman for goodness sake and she should be treated as such. Though, what was it about the thought of him treating her like a woman that had Kate's cheeks flaming an even deeper shade of red?

"Kate?" His gentle prompt brought her back to the room. "Would you like your bread buttered?"

"Oh, sorry, yes please. You are having one too, aren't you?"

"Sure." Cal hadn't been planning on it, but if eating

with her would put his guest at ease then he was certainly willing to do that. The dark circles under her eyes looked like sunken hollows in the shadowed light of the extractor hood. In case the bright glow of the kitchen light would hurt Kate's head, Cal had deliberately left the main bulb off.

Kate studied her host surreptitiously from below heavy eyelids, taking in the broad planes of his back beneath his t-shirt. She swallowed loudly and took a gulp of the water that Cal had kindly handed her before getting the bacon frying. *What's wrong with me?* she wondered silently. *I can't remember noticing any man in particular for the past five years, and now here I am wondering how his stubble would feel under my fingers.*

Bringing the sandwiches to the narrow bench, Cal took the stool next to her and they ate in companiable silence. Having eaten only one bowl of soup in the past twenty-four hours, Kate hadn't realised how much better she'd feel when she had something in her stomach. She wolfed it down, pausing only to chew as few times as possible.

"Wow, you made short work of that!" Cal smiled at her, the laughter lines on either side of his eyes clear at this close distance. He himself still had half to go. "Would you like another?"

"No, thank you though, I'd just better see how that settles before I try anything else!" Kate hoped he didn't think badly of her for eating so fast, then remembered he'd seen her out flat on the sofa in her cottage, drool running down her chin. Yes, this could only enhance the great image of her he must hold in his head!

Cal finished his food and turned to face Kate, who was already angled towards him. The stools were side by side, so that turning meant their knees were touching – bare knees, since they both wore shorts. At the skin to skin contact, Kate felt a strange electricity run up through her thighs. To be fair, it was the first friction of this kind that she'd had in many years, so she put the strange feeling down to that.

Cal tried to ignore his body's response to their close contact, and shuffled on his seat to make it less obvious. What power did this sweet woman have that she could turn him on just by touching her leg to his? Deciding he was clearly just a wee bit sex starved, Cal cleared his throat to speak and Kate looked at him expectantly.

Nothing. He had nothing. Couldn't form a coherent sentence. Instead, they simply kept looking at each other and smiling. Eventually, seeing the sky lightening through the blinds, Kate said,

"Well, would you mind if I take a shower before Josh wakes up?"

"A shower?" Cal swallowed down the squeak that his voice had become, wondering why he sounded seventeen again.

"Yes, I just haven't had..."

"Sorry, yes of course, I should have thought..."

"It's no bother, I just think I'd feel better if I..."

"Of course. I, um, I think I'll go on a run. Yes, that's it, a run is what I need!" Cal was muttering to himself now, as Kate was already at the sink rinsing the plates.

"Can you manage in the shower?" The moment the sentence was out and Kate spun round to look at him, her eyes round in surprise though her lips were trying to hold back a smile, Cal realised what that must have sounded like. "I just mean, without your stick, I hope I haven't offended..."

"Don't be silly!" Kate came around to stand beside his stool. "I can manage short bouts of standing, especially if I balance on one leg!" As if to demonstrate, Kate leant on her good leg. Unfortunately, her centre of gravity was still slightly knocked off by the previous day's medication, so she tottered unsteadily.

"Woah, there," Cal caught her elbow as she leaned into him. Looking up, Kate realised their faces were just inches apart. What was it with this man? It was as if she were attracted to him by some external force. *Can he feel it too?* she wondered.

Cal wasn't sure where to look. Half of Kate's torso now leant on his, her hair was against his neck and chin, and when she looked up at him with those gorgeous green eyes he couldn't think straight, all it would take would be for him to dip his head slightly…

SIXTEEN

Time stood still. Even the ticking of the kitchen clock seemed to be silenced. All that existed in the whole world was the two of them.

"Katie," it came out as a whisper as he dipped his head towards hers, but it had the effect of a bucket of freezing water thrown over Kate's body. Any passion that she had felt was gone in an instant and she pulled away abruptly.

"I'm sorry," Cal looked confused, he was sure he hadn't read the situation wrongly, but he was so out of touch with these things, that he knew it was quite possible he had. *She's a vulnerable guest in my home*, he mentally chastised himself.

"Don't worry about it!" Kate grabbed her stick from the wall beside the door and rushed to her room, keen he not see this next bout of tears. No one had called her that pet name since Patrick, and the shock of hearing it had taken her breath away. Kate could feel the panic rising, too quickly this time to give her the chance to use any of her strategies. She sank onto the bed and pulled her knees up to her chest, rocking back and forth as her breath came in unsteady gasps and the sobs stole what little oxygen she had.

"I forgot to give you some towels," Cal's voice at the door did nothing to halt her panic attack, in fact only making it worse. Kate couldn't speak to reply to him.

After a couple more knocks, the door was slowly pushed open and he poked his head around. "I'm so sorry to bother you, I just thought you'd need..." Cal stopped mid-sentence when he saw the state of her. "Oh sweetheart," he rushed to the bed, and without questioning his natural inclination, he sat down beside Kate and pulled her into his arms, right onto his lap, wrapping his arms around her gasping frame.

Kate didn't have the breath to argue, not that she wanted to. She felt safe, warm here from the moment he pulled her close, rubbing his hands over her back and whispering words of reassurance.

"You're okay, I've got you, try to breath slowly now, in - and - out, in - and - out..."

Kate focused on his words and the circular motion of his hand on her and after a few minutes her breathing had almost returned to normal. The tears still streamed, as did her nose, and she felt lightheaded, but she could breathe again. Then the shudders began, the familiar shakes which always followed an anxiety attack that was as quick and strong as this one had been. Far from questioning her as to this new development, Cal simply pulled her closer into his chest, kissing her head through her hair and speaking words of comfort. When he began to pray quietly, for Kate's breathing, her healing and her recovery, Kate didn't pull away. In fact, she sunk into the familiar words. It was a long time since she'd even been near a church, let alone sent a prayer heavenward, but somehow it felt right here and now, and with this gentle man.

The minutes past, Cal stopped speaking and focused on rubbing her back and brushing her hair from her wet face, and yet Kate still didn't feel the pull to move away from him.

"Thank you," she whispered into his chest, his t-shirt now damp from her tears.

"Please don't thank me," he replied, "it was me who upset you in the first place by almost kissing you out there."

"It wasn't the kiss," Kate spoke so softly, not making eye contact as she did so.

"Sorry?"

"It wasn't that which freaked me out. It was the name."

Cal tried to think back, hadn't he just used her own name?

"Katie," she continued, "it sent me back to… to a different time when I was a different person."

"Oh, I'm so sorry sweetheart," he tipped her chin gently with his index finger so that he could see her face, "I would never deliberately trigger any bad memories, I know… well, I know what that can be like."

Kate simply nodded. Cal couldn't possibly have known how something so simple would affect her, especially since she herself had been none the wiser until half an hour ago. The finger under her chin moved around to brush the tears from Kate's face and the man beside her smiled gently. It was impossible to not smile back, as weak and watery as the effect was.

"How did you know?" Kate broke the magic which was building between them once more.

"About what?"

"What to do… with me?"

"Oh, I…" Cal paused as memories flooded his consciousness. He and Sally in a doctor's room, her having a breakdown in this very room, a hospital bed… the images flashed through his mind as if on a movie reel.

"Hey, I'm sorry," It was Kate's turn now to look concerned and guilty, as she watched his eyes turn glassy and realised he'd disappeared inside his head. She ran her finger down his face from forehead to stubbled chin, before pulling it away just as quickly. The touch brought Cal back to the room, though and he blinked.

"Sorry, sweetheart, I, ah, I just have some experience with panic attacks."

"I understand." And she did.

The pair sat unmoving, she in his lap, he resting his chin on the top of her head, until they heard movement from the room next door, and Josh going into the bathroom. A look passed between them – they both knew this sweet moment of mutual compassion and comfort would have to end.

"I'll have my shower when he's gone to school," Kate whispered, "You two should just follow your normal weekday routine, don't let me delay you."

"Hey," Cal could feel her pulling away emotionally, and for some reason he felt desperate to hold onto their connection. His soul had finally found a kindred spirit and wasn't ready to let her disappear just yet. "Today's Friday, which means Cilla runs the café for me and I have the day off. Normally I do exciting things like the accounts and the housework, but today... well, why don't we do a wee bit of sightseeing?"

He looked so hopeful, and he had been so kind, how could she refuse? "That would be lovely, thank you... for everything."

"My pleasure," he whispered, unable to resist brushing his fingers once more through the wet curls which framed her face. Dropping a small, chaste kiss on her forehead, he helped Kate to her feet before leaving the room quietly.

Kate stood for a moment, unsure as to what had just

happened between them. It had been nothing. And everything. And she had no idea how to proceed now.

SEVENTEEN

The morning was freezing, but thankfully both the wind and the driving rain had decided to take a well-earned rest.

"We should take a stroll down to Connie's, to let her know how you're doing, then we'll go out in the car," Cal suggested, smiling when he saw Kate emerging from the bedroom. Her hair was still damp from her shower and her face still exceptionally pale, but her eyes seemed brighter than the previous day and she gave him such a smile, Cal felt moved to step just a little closer, so that he could smell the coconutty fragrance which wafted about her. They both hovered there, awkwardly, two almost-strangers who were somehow so much more than that.

"I'll grab my bag," Kate said, disappearing back into the bedroom. When she reappeared with both her handbag and her overnight bag, Cal felt an emotional pang. More of a pain, really. He wasn't ready for her to leave yet, though he admitted it to himself only reluctantly.

"Why don't you, ah, leave the holdall here?" he suggested, trying to appear nonchalant, though his heart hammered in his chest and he felt the blush spread across the bridge of his nose.

"Really? But we're walking past my…"

"I just meant, perhaps you should stay another night, we don't know whether you're fully better yet…"

"Well, I think I am…" Kate was about to say she felt fine – as fine as she ever did, anyway – when she realised that the thought of staying another night was actually quite appealing. Backtracking, she said, "I think I would like the knowledge there's someone there if I pass out again or anything, thank you, as long as it's no bother?"

Cal visibly relaxed, "Of course not, that's decided then," and before Kate could say another word he took the bag from her hand and returned it to the bedroom.

Hoping to have a quick visit with Constance was always a futile wish, Cal knew. You were lucky if you got out within the half hour, and if you accepted a cuppa... well, then you were in for the long haul! On this occasion, the old woman was so happy to see Kate up and about that she had the kettle on and the cake plated up before either he or Kate could refuse. Sitting together on her tiny settee, their thighs touching, the pair exchanged resigned smiles as they listened to her pottering about in the room next door. A large ginger tom cat appeared before them, as if conjured by magic, and Cal stiffened. He and Captain had a long history of abject hatred for one another which had moved from clawing and scratching to mutual mistrust. Kate looked from him to the cat and back again, trying to keep the amusement from her face. Upon spotting the new arrival, however, the heavy creature jumped immediately into her lap, leaving Cal scowling and Kate letting out an awkward giggle.

"Mangy traitor," Cal whispered, making Kate laugh out loud now.

"Ooh, what is this tomfoolery?" Constance asked, entering the room just at the moment Kate was trying to stifle a large snort as Captain hissed in Cal's direction before turning and purring at her. "Do you young uns have something to tell me?" She quirked an eyebrow, looking hopeful.

"Only that Kate is feeling better, and we're off out to Anstruther and then maybe Crail or St. Andrews for a look around and a bite to eat, if the weather holds off."

"Off out, eh?" The woman's girlish giggle and unsubtle wink left them both feeling a bit uncomfortable, so that an awkward silence ensued. With a final hiss towards Cal and a rub of his back against her palm, Captain vacated Kate's lap for a spot on the wide window sill.

"Anyway," Kate gulped down her tea and lemon drizzle cake, "I just wanted to thank you, Mrs. Auchterlonie, for helping me and looking after me so well."

"Tsshh it was nothing, lassie! You can come for your Sunday dinner and keep this old bird company to make up for it!"

"Oh, I, well, yes thank you." Kate realised she'd been outmanoeuvred yet again. This woman was a pro!

As they finally stood up to leave, after the fifth village anecdote, Connie grabbed Kate's hand and pulled her back as Cal left the room. "He's a good lad, that one, you know! You won't find better. Had a hard time these past few years, but the Good Lord saw him right so he did," she whispered.

"Ah, thank you, yes he seems lovely." Kate rushed out of the room, as fast as the cat at her heels and her walking stick would allow, her face flaming and her pulse beating loudly in her ears. *Was her attraction plain for everyone to see, or did Constance just have a sixth sense for these things? Perhaps it was just wishful thinking on the woman's part? Yes,* Kate decided, *that must be it.* Taking deep breaths, she waved to the old lady in the doorway and accepted Cal's offer to link her arm in his. For once, the freezing, salty air was a welcome balm to her burning face!

EIGHTEEN

Cal's ancient Volvo was certainly not a pretty vehicle, but it managed the steep twists and turns of the countryside roads without any bother. It was barely a ten minute drive along the coast to their first destination, Anstruther. Similar to Pittenweem, with its harbour and row of shops, Anstruther was the largest of the local fishing communities.

"There's a famous fish bar, does a cracking haddock and chips, if you fancy it?" Cal recommended as they strode arm in arm along the front street.

The seagulls seemed even louder here, as they ducked and dove above them, and there was a busyness about the place even in this quiet season. The pavement was narrow, and Kate was conscious of her limp and her cane, not wanting to trip anyone over or slow them down. Distracted, she didn't reply to Cal's question. Sensing her caution and wariness, Cal directed them across the road and onto a bench which faced the few boats still moored at this time of day. They sat down, quiet for a moment, until Kate spoke up,

"Thank you… again."

"What for?"

"Well for just now, sensing I needed a break, and for letting me stay. Everything."

"You know it's no bother," he turned to face her, "I couldn't have stayed away from you even if I tried, it's like a… a …." He struggled to find the right word.

"Magnet?"

"Yes, exactly, it's like a magnet that draws me to you, even when my head and any sense I've got tells me to leave it. Do you, ah… do you feel it too?" He felt his cheeks blush, ridiculous for a man in his forties he thought, and scrubbed at his face with gloved hands to hide his embarrassment.

"Thank you for being honest," Kate began, "It's one of the qualities I most admire in a person, in a friend," she

stopped speaking and Cal knew what she was saying –
he should back off. But then she continued, "I do feel it,
yes, strongly in fact. I don't know what it is either. I'm
not looking for a relationship, a holiday fling or
whatever people call it, I've sworn off men in fact…"
Realising she had probably said more than she'd
intended, Kate stood up, "Shall we get that fish and
chips, then?"

Cal had no idea where that left them. They both felt
drawn to each other, had admitted as much, but
neither wanted anything to come of it. *Or did he?* He
rushed after her, his mind bogged down in questions.

Haddock and chips with plenty of salt and vinegar was
just what the doctor ordered. That, along with the sea
air, had lifted Kate's spirits no end. It had nothing to
do with her earlier conversation with Cameron and his
admission that he felt drawn to her. Nothing at all.
They sat in companiable silence, back on their bench,
watching a fishing boat chug back into harbour, when
a white feather floated down and landed right in
Callum's lap. He picked it up and twirled it around
between thumb and finger.

"When my wife died," he began, "I was in no fit state
to look after myself let alone a nine year old boy, and

so the neighbours, friends and family helped out a lot. Constance, in particular, became his adopted grandmother. I remember one day he came home from some time with her, rushing through the front door and brandishing a feather just like this one. 'Dad, Dad,' he shouted, 'Granny Connie says it's a message from Mum! That a white feather suddenly appearing means your loved one is near you!' Well, I'd heard the old saying before of course, written it off as old wives' tales, stuff and nonsense, but seeing his little face all lit up for the first time since she'd gone, it touched me in here," he tapped his chest over his heart, and Kate tried to swallow down the lump in her throat. "Now, every time I see a feather – which is a lot since we've got all these seagulls," he looked wryly above their heads, to where three huge birds circled hungrily, hoping for the remains of their lunch, "I think of her being close still, and I'm comforted by it. Does that sound silly?" He looked directly at Kate, a questioning gaze, and she got the impression he was almost testing her, to see how much she truly understood.

"Of course it's not silly," Kate took his gloved hand in her own, aware of the tears he was trying to blink away discreetly. "It has long been said that St. Michael, the Archangel, sends feathers to comfort those in distress who call out to him."

"Really? I never heard that!" Cal smiled, genuinely grateful for her empathy.

"It's true. I think feathers are important too. When I was, ah, younger, the medication which I take for my anxiety wasn't sorted and I often felt either numb or distressed." She felt Cal stroking her palm with his thumb through their gloves. "I would sit at my favourite spot – a bit like this actually, overlooking the sea, but with the ruins of an ancient priory at my back – birds nested in the cliff ledges below. Often I would see feathers whipped up to me on the breeze, but they were taken away just as quickly, swirling and twirling in their flight. I used to think that catching a feather was as elusive as feeling happiness." Kate stopped and sniffed, suddenly emotional at the memory.

"And now, nowadays I mean, do you ever feel happiness?" Cameron asked softly, quirking the eyebrow closest to Kate.

"Well, I'm more stable as I'm better suited to my medication – I rarely have attacks like the one you saw yesterday, not that bad anyway – but as for happiness… yes, I feel it sometimes… Like when I'm with you." The last sentence was so quiet, it was almost drowned out by the noise of a particularly vociferous seagull.

"With me?" Cal needed confirmation, for his own heart's sake.

"Yes."

NINETEEN

When they pulled into the charming fishing village of Crail, with its cobbled streets and miniature harbour, Kate was transfixed by how pretty it was. Like Pittenweem, but even smaller, a little chocolate box of a village. They had a short walk around and then stopped outside a cute chocolate shop.

"Shall we have something to warm us up?" Cal asked.

"That sounds perfect," Kate didn't want to let on, but her leg and side were starting to ache, and her craving for painkillers was beginning to encroach on her reasonable thought process. She thought she could perhaps sneak a couple of capsules while he was ordering their drinks.

They pushed open the door to see that they were the only customers. The interior was done out like a Mediterranean café, all yellows and terracottas, but the tables were empty.

"Winter trade eh, Julie!" Cal commented as they found a cosy corner.

"Always the same, isn't it Cal? Thank goodness for the summer months! Come to check out the competition again?" They continued in friendly banter, Cameron introducing the woman to Kate, saying that she'd been one of Sally's best friends. For some reason, that made Kate uncomfortable – was she to be judged now? Would Julie assume she was his girlfriend? As the anxious paranoia began, Kate excused herself to use the bathroom. She swigged two Codeine Phosphate tablets at the ornate sink and splashed some cold water on her face.

When she emerged, Julie was busy behind the counter making their hot chocolates, and Cameron watched her keenly as she approached their table.

"Are you okay, sweetheart?" he enquired gently, "you've been a wee while…"

"Yes, thanks."

"Are you in pain from the walking?"

Could she not get anything past this guy? Kate contemplated being evasive, but knew he'd just keep digging. "Well, yes, I needed some pain relief." That would have to be enough.

"How much do you take in a day, Kate?" His eyes looked directly into hers, warm and not judgemental. But Kate was conditioned to expect criticism – from her parents and her colleagues, who were sick of her strange mood swings, her fatigue and unreliability. She had no idea what to say.

In the end, she simply stated, "Normally? Too many."

Cal reached out and took her hand across the table. Kate was tempted to pull away, worried what Julie would think, but the woman was paying them no attention, and the contact, especially now they were without gloves, was warm and welcome.

"And after the other night?"

He was like a dog with a bone, yet Kate couldn't turn away. "I got a scare, Cameron, so I've only had these two since then."

"Good, great, that's a great start. You know, there's a doctor at the local health centre, who looked after

Sally, a woman…"

"No!" And there it was, he'd found her limit. Kate had refused to see any doctor face to face for the past four years. She'd had enough of them and she wasn't about to change her mind now.

"Okay, that's okay," he rubbed a circle on her palm, calming, soothing.

"Two deluxe hot chocolates," Julie arrived with the huge drinks and Kate pulled her hand back abruptly, focusing on the tiny marshmallows and chocolate flakes which she prodded with her spoon, determined not to look into the eyes of the kind man whose gaze she felt heating her own face.

The drive home seemed to take a lot longer, and Kate dozed off in the passenger seat. Cal looked across at her pretty face, her lashes fanned out over high cheekbones, and wondered what on earth he was going to do. He had already shared more with her than anyone since his bereavement, he felt a connection and knew she did too. But what of it? Who would want a broken middle-aged man, a single dad at that? Could he even have a relationship – was he capable of loving so completely again now that he knew what true heartbreak felt like? Question piled upon question, but no answers came forward.

As they drove into Pittenweem Kate awoke, momentarily unsure where she was. Then she smelled his fresh woody scent, looked across from eyelids only half open, and saw Cal at the wheel, his brow creased in thought. His floppy brown hair was tousled from their day outdoors and his stubble was even thicker now. Something inside her did a little flip and Kate tried to fight the attraction, to deny it so that it ceased to be true. To no avail. Sighing, she sat up a little and caught her companion's attention.

"Hey beautiful," the words were out before Cal could catch them back, said on impulse without thinking.

He blushed a fine shade of beetroot which gave Kate a small smile.

"Hey, you," she replied, trying to put him back at ease. "So, will Josh be home from school by now?"

"No, he normally just meets me at the church hall on alternate Fridays. We'll head straight there."

"The church hall?" Kate didn't like where this was heading.

"Yep, I run a film night there every other week for the young people. Keeps them out of trouble!" Cal pulled into a tiny car park outside the parish church as he winked at Kate.

The gesture did nothing to calm her nerves. A church. Once a place of sanctuary, now a reminder of a past best forgotten.

"I'll walk back down to my cottage," she said abruptly, and tried to make a hasty exit from her side. Cal was quicker though, of course he was, not having a stick and dodgy limb to contend with, and he helped her out gently.

"Why? I thought you were staying with us again?" he tried not to sound whiny or needy, but his stomach was doing a flip and his heartrate had accelerated once more.

"I just… I just don't do churches, okay? Not my thing."

"Okay, well we'll just be in the church hall and once I set it going and they're all quiet we can pop home for a cuppa, or the pub if you fancy a drink?"

He was so endearing, with his big, hopeful eyes, that Kate found him impossible to refuse. "Okay, lead the way then," she said, making it clear in her tone that she did so reluctantly.

Cal reached across and took her spare hand, smiling, "Thank you," he whispered, and Kate felt slightly placated, though her stomach was still in knots and the nausea of the day before had returned full force.

TWENTY

Of all the days for the projector to not work, it had to be this one! Cal lamented silently as he tried to get the stupid thing set up. The hall was half full of sweaty, rowdy teenagers, not to mention the few old folk who also often joined them for a free night out. Tonight's film was 'Gremlins', and apparently the oldie was a popular choice. If it would only work. Pausing to take a deep breath and let some of his frustration dissipate, Cal's eyes searched the room for Kate. He'd asked Josh to introduce her to a few people, but the lad was with his mates, engrossed in a conversation about the X-Box. He scanned the room and began to panic slightly when he couldn't find her. She wouldn't have taken off by herself, would she? It was dark, and the path into the centre of the village was a hilly slope. He focused back on the task at hand, the sooner he got this damn film started, the sooner he could go look for her.

Kate had only meant to pop to the ladies, to have another tablet to calm her nerves. Then she'd ended up in the large kitchen, looking for a glass of water for her dry throat. It smelled like all the church kitchens she'd been in, slightly musty, foisty and of stale food. Somehow choosing the wrong door back out of the room, Kate found herself in a small corridor, at the end of which she could see the chapel itself, illuminated by small electric candles around the walls. Her feet seemed to have a mind of their own, and Kate was drawn to the scene. Her entry brought her in behind and to the side of the alter, at the other end to the main church doors. Walking on silent feet, even her cane making no noise on the thin carpet, she made her way around to the first pew and sat gingerly down.

"What am I even doing here?" she asked aloud, knowing she would not receive an answer.

The pulpit itself was very old, dark wood, with simple lines and a strong, no nonsense look. Upon it sat a large bible, open at some random page. All so strange and so familiar at the same time. Kate didn't even realise she was crying until the salty taste met her lips and she brushed the tears away angrily. This was why she didn't want to set foot in a church. It made things worse. Where was God when you needed him? Standing up to go back the way she'd come, Kate spotted the familiar green coat of Cal as he stood watching her from the small doorway. How long had he been there? He must think her ridiculous, the amount of crying she'd done since they met. Unstable. Unhinged even. Kate sat back down with a thud and put her head in her hands. It was all too much.

Cal tried to hide his surprise at finding Kate in this main part of the church, though he was certainly relieved she hadn't left the building altogether. Walking slowly he sat down on the pew beside her, wanting nothing more than to pull her to him and comfort her, but instead leaving a respectable distance between them. When a few minutes had passed without a word, just the sound of her muffled sobs, Cal began to pray in his head, for this woman who was in pain, that she be released from her past traumas, that she find peace and healing. His lips moved to his silent pleas, but no sound came out, yet he turned to find Kate staring at him.

"I was just praying for you. Sorry." Cal felt like he should apologise as she looked fairly angry, though he actually felt no remorse asking for his Father's hand on her.

"Umhm, let's get out of here," Kate grabbed her bag and her stick and stood up. Taking one last look at the bible and the large wooden cross straight ahead, she waited for Cal to move out of the pew so that she could leave. Except he didn't budge. In fact, he remained seated, looking up at her.

"Why don't you talk to me about it?" he asked gently, "It might help. You don't act as someone who's never in their life experienced faith or redemption."

Kate stood with her spare hand on her hip and regarded him for a moment. What he was asking was no easy favour. Reluctantly, she sat back down on the cold wooden bench, turning slightly to face her companion. Seeing the emotional effort it took her, Cal shuffled closer and took her hand in his. Nothing was said for the next minute or so, as Kate collected her thoughts, distracted by the feeling of his hand on hers. When she eventually spoke, it was more of a harsh whisper,

"You're right, I have known God in my life. And it's true what they say – He gives and He takes away!"

"Isn't that the truth!" Cal was pensive and she knew he drew his understanding from his own painful life experience. "But what He offers," he continued softly, "the promise of forgiveness and redemption, and an eternal life with Him, is that not worth the price? Hasn't Christ paid the ultimate price for us first?"

Kate didn't want to outright contradict him, as she knew he must have suffered gravely when his wife died, just as she had with Patrick, even more so. And deep down, she knew of Jesus' love for her, but she could just not face the contradictions in her faith any more. Sensing she did not want to discuss it further, Cal suggested they drive down into the village centre for a drink,

"We can have a wee dram in the Bonnie Scotsman, if you like?"

"Thank you for the offer, but I find alcohol doesn't mix well with my meds. Would a coffee from the shop be possible? I mean, I know it's closed now, but you must have owner's perks, right?" She flashed him a watery smile and Cal knew in that moment that he would have granted her whatever she asked.

"You've got it!" he said, standing up and offering her his arm, "I might even throw in a slice of cake if you're lucky!" He had barely scratched the surface with this intriguing woman, he knew, and he was keen to find out more. *All in good time*, he told himself, *all in good time.*

TWENTY-ONE

The ever-reliable Cilla had cleaned and locked up the shop, so when the pair entered all was calm and quiet. Cameron flicked on the lights and indicated one of the stools at the counter, "Hop up, My Lady, and tell me what your heart desires!"

Blushing at his flirty banter, Kate did as he asked and made herself comfortable whilst Cal switched on the industrial coffee machine. The smell of coffee beans filled the air and she drew in an appreciative breath.

"I wish all my local customers were as appreciative as you," Cal smiled as he set about preparing two espressos, "the most adventurous many of them get is a filter coffee with cream!"

Kate laughed, explaining how she herself only used to drink herbal teas – fruit, chamomile, peppermint – not turning to coffee until… here she paused, not wanting to mention the accident and spoil the light-hearted mood. Cal helped her out, giving her an incredulous look and exclaiming,

"You? Without coffee? Now that's a scary prospect!"

"Cheeky!" Kate replied, accepting her cup eagerly and taking a strong smell of the delicious aroma. When a piece of apple pie appeared beside her, she smiled up into Cal's face gratefully.

Taken aback by the first completely open smile he had seen from his beautiful guest, Cal stood open-mouthed for a moment, simply staring.

"If the wind changes, you'll stay like that!" Kate nudged him gently in the ribs with her elbow, treating him to one of her mother's favourite sayings.

"Ah, now you sound like Connie!" Cal shook off the feeling of intense attraction as best he could and took the seat next to her.

"Dis pie id delicious!" Kate spoke around a huge mouthful.

"You can thank Cilla for that, she's a fantastic baker –

you should see what she'll have stored in the pantry
for the weekend custom!"

"Ooh, don't tempt me!" Kate's words hung in the air,
as if they were charged with a double meaning. They
looked at each other over the rim of their coffee cups,
with smiling eyes, until Cal lowered his drink slowly
to the table. Without saying a word… not trusting
himself to say a word… he leant forward and ran the
back of his knuckles gently over Kate's cheek.

Kate knew she should break the moment with a joke,
or a quick peck of his palm and then gently remove it,
but she did neither. Instead, she sat stock still, staring
from his eyes to his lips and back again,
subconsciously licking her own lips as she did so. The
jolt of electricity from his skin touching hers was a
welcome feeling – of being alive and desired.

"Kate?" Her name on his mouth was nothing more
than a whisper, a question, a request. She was grateful
for his old-fashioned respectfulness, but could only
nod in return. The butterflies in her stomach, which
she thought had died with that old her, had
resurrected themselves in full force and now fluttered
away, making her feel slightly nauseous with both
excitement and nerves.

Cal knew that this was his make or break moment with

the beautiful woman who had come into his life so suddenly, turning his commitment to celibacy on its head. He would either connect with Kate on a level she hopefully couldn't deny, or scare her away once and for all. He dipped his head slowly, maintaining the eye contact which neither seemed able to break. Cal looked for any sign that she was pulling away, either mentally or physically. As he saw none, his lips continued on their trajectory until so softly, barely touching, they met hers.

Kate made a small gasp at the tiny touch. He had barely touched his lips to hers, resting there without any friction, and she already felt him in her heart. Rubbing her mouth slightly against his warm one, Kate welcomed the resulting frisson which ran through her body. Clearly experiencing the same feeling, Cal pressed his mouth more firmly against hers, testing her response. For once, Kate's mind ceased its whirling, she stopped second guessing everything, and just let herself feel, responding in kind to the beautiful pressure he exerted on her.

Cal reined himself in. The desire to taste her, to comfort her, to reassure her he was here for the long haul was almost overwhelming, but he needed Kate's reassurance too. That she accepted, welcomed his kiss. That it meant more to her than a passing flirtation.

Completely vulnerable, he felt like he was on a cliff edge. Desperately not wanting to step back, but also afraid to make the leap.

Their bodies made the decision for him, mouths merging, caution being gradually replaced by hunger, until both were left dizzy and breathless. Reluctantly, Kate pulled away, only an inch or so, still able to feel his warm breath on her face. Cal took both her hands in his, their knees touching, eyes glued to the other's. She took but a second to regroup, then, needing to feel him again, she leant in and captured Cal's mouth with hers once more. He moved one hand to cup her cheek, and the other trailed through her windswept curls. Kate angled her face into his palm, not breaking contact with his mouth, and let out a small moan of pleasure.

Cal couldn't help himself. His body, long starved of the affection only a partner could give, had a mind of its own. He needed to touch her, feel her. Dotting kisses from Kate's soft mouth, along her jawline and to her ear, he felt her breath hitch as he whispered,

"You are so beautiful, so sweet, you're everything my mind didn't realise my heart was praying for."

"Oh Cal," Kate turned her head so that their mouths were now level again, placing her hand over his which still cupped her face. "I don't know that I'm ready for a relationship, you've seen how I am, how brok…" His finger over her lips stopped Kate mid-sentence.

"Shh, please stop speaking of yourself like that. Some of us are just as tempered by our past, it's just not so visible to the eye. But we all deserve to be loved… and you are so easy to love." Cal hadn't intended to make such a declaration. His mouth had spoken the words before his brain kicked in. He pulled away, scared to see her reaction.

Kate froze for a moment. This was going too fast, her heart was beating a quickstep in her chest and her senses still whirled from his touch. Part of her, instinctively, wanted to pull her face away from his hand, but the other half, which surprised her, kept her hand over his, locking it in place. Neither moved as she formulated her response.

"You are surely an easy man to love, too, Cameron McAllister," she whispered, "but I'm not sure I'm capable of giving any man what he needs. I fell far short of that the last time I tried."

Cal gave her a sweet kiss on the lips, short and brief, but just as scorching to Kate's soul, before replying, "I can't say whether that is true, or whether you're just being hard on yourself again, sweetheart, but what I do know is that a lot depends on how well you connect as people. We often can't give what others need if we aren't being fulfilled by them in return."

Kate took a moment to think about this. Lifting her hand from his, as his thumb ran small circles over her cheek bone, Kate tipped forward so that their foreheads were touching, and her fingers ran absentmindedly through his thick hair. She had not considered things from this angle before. Certainly, she knew she hadn't met any of Patrick's needs – physical or emotional – but had he met hers? Definitely food for thought.

Sensing she had retreated into her memories, and not wanting to probe further, Cal laced his fingers through Kate's against his hair.

"I should be going down to clear up and fetch Josh," he said, the reluctance clear in his voice, "how about I run you a bath so you can have a nice soak whilst I'm gone?"

To her aching limbs, the offer sounded heavenly, and was certainly too tempting for Kate to refuse. Helping her down from the high counter stool, Cal guided her gently up the stairs to the flat before disappearing to the bathroom. Hearing the bath running, Kate tried to ignore the trembling in her hand and the ache in her heart. Whatever happened now, she had the potential to hurt this lovely man, and she could not bear the thought of that.

TWENTY-TWO

Cal pulled into the car park at the church with an unnecessary squeal of tires. His mind raced and he wanted to be as quick as possible, worried that Kate would fall trying to get out of the tub. She had reassured him that she was fine, as she moved passed him into the tiny bathroom, but he couldn't help but want to make sure she was okay. Seeing Josh hovering in the church foyer, a look of impatience on his young face, Cal hurried over.

"Where've you been, dad? My friends have gone, even the old folks who were snoring through most of it have set off home!"

"I'm sorry, son. There was… something in the shop I

had to tend to." It was only a fib, more a lie of omission, Cal told himself. Though he hated not being honest with the lad.

"Hmmph. Well I've put the projector away and cleared up the crisp packets. Old Mr. Emery washed the cups and glasses and left them on the drainer."

"Aw, you're a good lad. I'll make sure you have some extra tuck money for school."

"And maybe Evan could come round tomorrow to play on the X-Box?"

"Go on then. You can text him, if his mum drops him over when I'm in the shop, I'll take him back after tea."

The boy perked up immediately, and Cal was grateful for his son's simple requests. *Long may it continue*, he thought, *before life gets difficult for him as it inevitably does*.

Cal checked the church hall and locked up while Josh waited in the car. He could not switch off his thoughts of Kate, and was preoccupied when he returned to the vehicle.

"Has she gone now?" Josh asked, as if reading his mind.

"Who, son?"

"The woman, the strange one who stayed over."

"She's not strange, Josh, just… quiet." Cal struggled to find a description which encompassed Kate whilst hiding his interest in her.

"Do you like her?" Since when had his little boy become so astute?

"She seems lovely," Cal tried to be as vague as possible, but could feel the heat rising up his neck.

"Hmmph, it's better when it's just the two of us," Cal looked over to see Josh peering at him inquisitively, looking for some tell-tale sign of something Cal didn't want to reveal.

"You'll always be my top priority, son," Cal tapped Josh's knee affectionately and changed the subject to food, something he knew was normally always on his growing son's mind, "Shall we stop for a fish supper at Nancy's?" This was their Friday night routine – cod and chips from the local fry place. Cal had hoped to go straight home for once, but he knew Josh would get suspicious if they didn't stick to the plan.

"Aye, and a can of pop?" His hopeful face reminded Cal of the chubby toddler his son had been, and he was suddenly overcome with emotion. So many memories. No one left to share them with. Visions of Sally drifted through his mind – earlier, happier ones, before she became sick. And he felt a guilt that sliced through him at his thoughts of Kate, at the fact he could still smell and taste her. How could he have betrayed Sally so badly?

Kate spent a blissful half an hour soaking her weary body, trying to keep her mind on the book she'd brought and to stop it drifting back to Cal. His warm brown eyes, hair greying at the temples, the feel of his hands in her hair and his mouth on hers. She sighed contentedly as she pulled on her pyjamas – no point getting dressed again this late in the day – and a dressing gown which she found on the back of the bedroom door. It smelled of him, and she held the sleeve to her nose, glad there was no one to witness her embarrassing action. Just as she was coming out of the room and into the living area, Cal and Josh returned, their heavy footfall on the stairs and their laughter making Kate suddenly feel as if she were an intruder in their home. She hovered gingerly in the doorway to the communal kitchen diner, as Josh burst into the room, stopping short when he saw her there.

"Ah, Kate's staying another night," Cal realised too late that he hadn't actually mentioned that fact in the car, when he should have.

"Umhm," Josh had returned to the usual teenage grunting, and Cal was sad for a moment that their banter had ended. Seeing Kate standing there though, clearly unsure of herself, and in his robe, had his heart beating faster and his senses reeling once more. Apparently his body hadn't got the memo from his head, that he should be backing off and remembering his wife. *My dead wife*, Cal thought sombrely.

"We've brought supper," he tried to force a smile, "Sorry, it's the same we had at dinner time. Different fish, though…" he realised he was prattling, and she simply stood there, propped against the kitchen bench now, wringing her hands together. He couldn't help it, Cal found his legs walking him up to her, standing just out of reach, until he leant forwards and took her hands in his to stop their anxious movements. Thankfully, Josh had taken his food, still in the paper with no plate, and hot-footed it to his room. Ordinarily, Cal would've made him come back to eat it on a plate at the table, but tonight he figured it was better if the boy wasn't around to see his father make a fool of himself.

Kate looked into the worried eyes, so distant when Cal had arrived home, and now fixed on her again. He held her hands, rubbing his thumbs over and around, and Kate was rendered immobile. They stared at each other, as if trying to work out the answer to some unfathomable riddle, until eventually Cal whispered, "Let's have this before it gets cold."

He grabbed some plates from the cupboard behind her, reaching over her so that Kate could have moved ever so slightly to the right and kissed him... *Pull yourself together*, she mentally rebuked herself before limping as fast as her leg would let her to the table.

Cal checked his phone for the umpteenth time, shielding the glare in case it woke Josh who was on the top bunk. It was unlikely though, since his son's snoring ricocheted around them like tiny bugs bouncing off the bed posts. Quarter past one. Was she still awake? Had she lain awake thinking of him, as much as he was thinking of her? A mixture of guilt and longing rolled around in Cal, until he felt sick with it. He stood up slowly, stretching his bent limbs. He would certainly be glad to get his bed back, though the knowledge that that would mean her leaving tomorrow made him sad. He intended to go to the kitchen, Cal promised himself, but the light under her door stopped him in his tracks.

Kate couldn't sleep and was fighting the craving for painkillers. She could see him in her mind, smell him all around her, heightening her senses until slumber was impossible. She'd grabbed her sketchpad and decided to draw, shocked when his features appeared unbidden on the blank sheet. She could remember every detail from Cal's slightly bushy eyebrows to his once-broken nose. She sketched his hair flopping over his forehead, reaching eyes so warm she lost herself in them. Hearing a tap on the door, Kate shoved the book under the blanket, as if she'd been caught doing something inappropriate.

"Come in," her voice sounded croaky and strange even to herself.

Cal couldn't believe what he was doing, yet he seemed to have lost all control of his senses. Like a moth to a flame, he opened the door at the sound of Kate's voice and tiptoed into the room, shutting it lightly behind him.

TWENTY-THREE

He walked straight to her, propelled by some invisible force which had a complete disregard for propriety. Kate could not take her eyes from his, accepting his approach, the inevitability of it.

"Hey," Cal whispered, hovering at the side of the bed, thankful his good sense had returned just long enough to stop him crawling in beside her.

"Hey," Kate whispered back, shuffling over so he could join her. It was a silent invitation, but one which spoke volumes. Cal lifted the duvet and slid underneath, careful not to touch her bare legs.

"I…" he paused, unsure how to explain it. Honesty won out, "I needed you."

It was said so simply, yet it encompassed so many of the feelings which Kate shared. She nodded mutely, smiling in understanding.

Cal felt himself relax slightly at her response. Without words, he lifted the arm closest to her, and Kate shuffled her body against his, nestling her head in the crook of his shoulder. It felt so right. Minutes passed and neither spoke, but silence was no longer uncomfortable between them. Eventually, out of nowhere, Cal heard himself begin talking, "I loved her, my wife," he felt himself blush at the admission and wondered why he had chosen to mention Sally now. Was it to stop himself taking this any further?

"I know," Kate had seen the grief in his face when they met, understood a little of what he had suffered. "She must have been a very special woman."

"She was." It was true, Sally had been that and more. And yet Cal wanted to be with Kate so badly. He longed for her touch in a way he'd thought no woman would reach him again.

"You must miss her badly," Kate ventured, her interest genuine.

"In the beginning, it was like losing a limb, like having my heart ripped out," Cal shifted so that he could look

Kate in the eyes as he spoke, "I was exhausted from the battle we'd been though, worried for Josh, unable to grieve properly for myself and what I'd lost."

Kate nodded, "I think I understand. And now? Has it gotten any better?"

Cal thought for a moment before he replied, trying to be as honest as possible both to himself and to her, "It was, I had put it in a box marked 'Sally' in my mind and only opened it on the days I was emotionally strong enough. Eventually, over time, the box didn't dig into my heart quite so painfully, it just rested there, part of me but no longer a heavy burden. But now, since I met you, I feel like…" he struggled to form the sentence.

Kate waited, patiently, desperate to reach out and touch him, to comfort him, but she held back.

"Now, I worry that I'm betraying her. I feel… guilty," he whispered, "Yet I can't help myself. I need you." His eyes became glassy, though no tears were shed, and Cal looked at the woman he had just bared his soul to, torn.

Unable to stop herself, Kate reached out and cupped his cheek in her palm, feeling his rough stubble and hard jawline. "I was engaged to be married," she said suddenly, surprising herself, "but we weren't close. Me, I was the problem. My mental health issues, my inability to be… physically close to him. I wanted to wait till marriage, but it wasn't as simple as that – I was just numb to life, I think. My body, my senses, had shut down." She paused, studying Cal intently, searching for any hint of rejection in his features. Confident she saw none, Kate continued, "We booked a last chance break, to try to salvage the relationship. And he died. Because of me. And now I'm broken, too broken." She stopped there, her hands back in her lap, wrung together like she was squeezing the water out of a dishcloth.

Cal's heart broke for the pain he saw on Kate's face and heard in her voice. He reached out and took both her hands in his, bringing them up to his mouth and kissing her white knuckles. "Aw sweetheart," he whispered, wanting to reassure her that she couldn't have been to blame for her fiancé's death, that a relationship takes two, that she was certainly not broken and unlovable – so many trite responses, so he just stayed silent.

"It was an accident. On the motorway. We were headed here, five years ago this week." Kate's voice broke in a sob. It wasn't necessary for her to describe it further, as unbeknown to her, Cal had already seen her sketched pictures of the event, graphic in their detail. He snuggled her closer into him, resting his chin on her head. Why she had chosen to come to the very place which reminded her most of the accident, he couldn't fathom, yet he was certainly thankful that she had been led back to the village.

"I've got you, let it all out," he said, as Kate shuddered beneath the force of her tears, clinging to him as to a life raft.

As the sobs subsided, and she looked up at him, Kate saw the tears in Cal's eyes, too. They had both loved and lost, both were unsure if they could do so again. But where did that leave them?

TWENTY-FOUR

Kate snuggled as close as she could, and they both shuffled down a bit so they were lying down properly. Both processed their own thoughts silently, minds whirring as they refused to break the physical bond they were sharing – her arm across his waist, his arm around her, no air between their torsos. Eventually, Cal sighed and spoke,

"I'm not sure where that leaves us?" It was a question filled with desperation, resignation and a little splash of hope.

"Me neither," Kate whispered.

The reluctant acknowledgement that a shared future was very much uncertain weighed heavily, and served only to make them savour the physical connection more acutely – just in case it was their last.

"I can't think straight right now," Cal admitted, we probably should put some space between us to work out how we feel… from tomorrow, I mean," he added quickly, feeling her body stiffen.

"Yes, that sounds sensible," Kate whispered, tilting her face to look at him.

They were caught once again in each other's eyes – deep pools of reflected longing.

"Stay with me," she had no idea where the confidence to say it had come from, but Kate felt no regret, "I can't, I mean, I'm not a one night stand, Cameron, so no sex. But… hold me?"

Cal breathed out the breath he'd been holding. He hadn't wanted to leave her, to get out of this bed with no guarantee of kissing her again. He could live without sex, heck he'd done it for long enough. But to get through this night without her touch? He didn't think that would be possible.

"Thank you, yes of course… Definitely no sex," he reassured her, winking to try to lighten the mood, "Let's just be close, shall we?"

"Perfect," Kate couldn't drag her eyes from his lips as he spoke, a fact that had not gone unnoticed. Cal leant down and grazed her mouth with his, feeling her immediate response, then pulled away, suddenly unsure of himself.

"Kiss me," Kate whispered, her mouth a hairsbreadth from his. Taking the lead, she kissed Cal with a passion she had felt but not yet shared with him. His surprise was soon overtaken by his need, and she felt the force of their embrace right down to her toes. The material of their nightwear suddenly seemed an unwelcome barrier, and Kate wondered what it would feel like to have his hands on all of her.

Legs entwined, hands touching hair and faces, they poured all of their desire into that kiss, worried it would be one of the few they would share.

"Sorry about him, he has a mind of his own," Cal paused to whisper, directing a rueful look at his crotch.

Kate giggled, at ease with this gorgeous man who was treating her like fine china. Suddenly, not wanting to be thought of as fragile any longer, she took Cal's face in her hands and kissed him with a ferocity that shocked them both. Their mouths merged together easily, as if they belonged that way, until eventually Cal pulled away, "Wow, sweetheart, we may need to calm down a bit," his face was shadowed in the lamplight, his eyes hooded and sultry, and Kate was so aroused she could only nod in response. Shifting, she snuggled into his shoulder once more, and he brought both arms around her, pulling her as close as possible. Feeling content and at peace for the first time in as long as she could remember, Kate's eyes drifted shut and she dozed off, with Cal quickly following suit.

When he awoke several hours later, Cal immediately noticed that they had shifted in their sleep, both now lying on their sides, and Kate was plastered against his back, with her hand slung across his waist pinning him to her. Cal held his breath a moment, trying to calm his racing heart. The feeling of waking up next to her was more intense than he'd expected, and he dared not move for fear of her pulling away from him.

You fool, Cal thought, *as soon as morning comes, not only will she leave your bed, but possibly your life too. She'll squirrel herself away again for the rest of her stay and it'll be like you're strangers!* The thought left Cal with a feeling akin to seasickness, deep in his gut. It was all too quick, though, he knew. The rational part of him accepted that time and space were needed. But his heart, well that was a different matter.

"What are you thinking? Your back is so tense!" he felt

Kate nuzzle into him as she spoke, her words muffled by his t-shirt.

"Sorry to wake you, sweetheart," he dodged the question, turning onto his back, so that she could cuddle across his chest once more. Newly nestled into him, Kate reached her hand up to his face, tracing the outline of his lips in the half-light.

"It's some time to think, that's all," it was as if she could read his thoughts, "maybe we'll both decide we can make a go of it?"

The 'maybe' hung in the air and worried them both, but neither mentioned it further, instead both sought comfort in the other's lips again. Morning would come, far too soon, but for now they had each other.

TWENTY-FIVE

Kate trudged wearily down the street to Connie's door.
The past twenty-four hours, since leaving Cal's, had
been slow and emotional. She had fought, and
thankfully won, the battle with her body, which craved
painkillers and almost drove her mad. She had
succumbed to paracetamol every six hours, and
codeine just three times. A huge win in her book. No
sleeping tablets either, as she'd lain awake thinking of
her one wonderful night with Cal. Kate couldn't
remember ever sleeping better than when she was in
his arms, even though they had only managed a few
hours of real sleep in the end. Nevertheless, she had
felt rested and alert on Saturday morning. As he'd left
the bed early, keen to not let Josh find him there,

although the lad always slept late on the weekend anyway, Cal's absence had left a cold spot in more than just the mattress.

They had eaten a breakfast of toast and eggs, before Cal had to go down and get the coffee shop open. Nothing had been said, although the occasional brushing of hands and meeting of glances told them they were both equally sad to be parting. They had swapped mobile numbers and then, ever the gentleman, Cal had of course offered to walk her home. Kate had stubbornly refused, instead shuffling back down the lane dejectedly.

How could a man I've known for less than a week have this effect on me? Kate wondered as she tapped lightly with the lions-head knocker. Captain, at his sentry place on the windowsill, watched her impassively as she listened to Constance's footsteps coming along the hallway. The door was pulled open with a force which belied the older woman's tiny stature, and Kate was enveloped in a warm hug,

"There you are, lassie, I was listening out for ye! The roast's almost ready, it's so grand to have someone to cook for…"

Kate smiled her greeting, as she couldn't get a word in edgewise. Led by the hand into the sitting room, she took a seat on the sofa, remembering the last time she had sat here, with Cal. Captain graced her with his presence on her lap, and Connie took the wing-backed chair opposite. A low fire crackled in the hearth, surrounded by a myriad of ornaments, and Kate felt herself begin to relax in the cosy surroundings.

"I went to the early service this morning," Connie launched into a minute-by-minute recap of her church visit, and Kate let the words wash over her gently.

"So," Connie paused eventually and looked at her inquisitively, her head cocked to one side like a curious owl, "You stayed with Cameron for two nights then?" It was more a statement than a question. *The village gossip train must have had full steam ahead on this one*! Kate thought grudgingly.

"Yes, he was worried I'd have another… lapse."

"Ah, a thoughtful lad that one. So, you and he got along nicely?" She was about as subtle as a brick.

"Very well, yes" Kate could feel the heat across her cheeks and down her neck. She had already removed her coat and scarf, so attributed it to the fire. It had nothing at all to do with the memories flashing unbidden through her mind, of course.

"And when will ye be seeing him again? Apart from our elevenses tomorrow…" Constance added quickly.

"Um, I'm not sure, I mean I should be painting…"

"Pah, there's plenty o' time for that!"

Thankfully, the sound of a pan bubbling over drove Connie back to the kitchen, and Kate stepped into the small room to help her plate up. A round table sat in the centre, laid out beautifully with a white, lace-edged tablecloth and silver cutlery.

"You shouldn't have gone to so much bother," Kate felt touched by the effort the older woman had made on her account.

"Not at all. It's so rare to have someone to share a meal with…" For the first time since she'd met her, Kate heard Connie's voice wobble, and she turned away slightly so as not to see the tears which the woman was desperately trying to blink away.

Roast dinner demolished, topped off by home-made trifle, Kate sat on the settee with her cup of tea, quite unable to move. She wished she'd worn elasticated leggings rather than her skinny jeans, which she struggled to unbutton. Keen to listen rather than do any talking, she initiated a conversation which she knew would get Connie talking,

"So, Constance, tell me about your family…"

"Well, lassie, there's just me now, but there used to be five of us. Can you imagine? Five of us in this wee cottage? Of course, when we all lived here the children were just little. I lost my Albert you see," she paused and pointed to a black and white photo on the mantle, while Kate tried to swallow the lump in her throat, "when little Billy was only ten, and the twins, Linda and Leslie, just four. He was a bonnie man, my Bertie, and a dedicated fisherman. Knew the sea like the back of his hand. Until the day it caught him unawares, and a storm took his whole ship out. There's a plaque on one of the benches in the harbour, I'll show you if you like?" Kate could only nod, as she tried to control her emotional response to the story. Connie herself seemed unaffected.

"Anyway, it hit us all bad, the whole community. Four good men gone to meet their Maker. Four families left bereft. It hit my Billy the hardest, just at the age when a lad needs a dad to guide him, about the same age as little Josh down the road was… anyway, he went off the rails the moment those hormones hit. Just small stuff at first, cigarettes, then alcohol, and later, when he ran away at sixteen, I learnt he'd turned to the hard stuff, those bad drugs and such. We tried to find him, but he didn't want to be found. Simple as that. I got a call three years after he disappeared, from a girl I didn't know, telling me to hot foot it to the hospital in Dundee. He'd overdosed, you see. They tried to save him, of course, and he was in a coma for five weeks, before we had to make the decision to turn the machines off. Worst day of my life, up there with hearing from the harbourmaster that the lifeboats were comin' in empty handed after the storm." She stopped and took a thoughtful sip of her tea. Kate wondered how the woman could be so stoic.

As if in answer, Connie said, "I've shed enough tears for a lifetime lassie, and only my faith has kept me going. Even when I walked away, He walked alongside me. Especially since the girls left."

"They didn't...?"

"Die too?" Connie give her a wry smile, "No, but there was nothing to keep them here but a grieving mother, so they upped sticks, one to Brisbane and one to Banff. All the B's!" She giggled at her own joke, before suddenly becoming sombre again. "We talk the last Sunday of the month, on that Skype, Cameron lets me use his computer," she sucked her cheeks in for a moment, as if stuffing down the desire to say more, "Anyways, I have happy memories and sad ones. It's the happy ones I choose to focus on."

Kate nodded, her knuckles white where she gripped her mug tightly, having the impression that this small, unassuming old lady was trying to tell her something. The tale had certainly made her think – Why had her faith not withstood the test? Why couldn't she focus on the good memories, what few there were, of her time with Patrick? Perhaps because Connie did not blame herself, she was free of the guilt-ridden self-loathing that Kate was mired in? It added a new dimension to Kate's thought process, which was already a multi-layered confusion of questions with no answers.

TWENTY-SIX

The next day was Monday, and Kate awoke early, positioning herself out on the pavement facing the Firth, as she had been that first morning when Cal had bumped into her. She told herself repeatedly that it was not in the hope of seeing him, not at all, but the words didn't ring true even in her own ears. The wind blew into her face, gathering sand and dust from the rocks below, and she shaded her eyes against its onslaught. Even though they had now entered March, the weather was still the frigid cold of a winter not ready to release its grip on the Scottish coast.

Kate shivered and pulled on the tartan blanket which lay over her knees. She looked at the painting which she seemed to have done on autopilot. It was a man's

face, from a side profile, but this time it wasn't
Cameron. It was Patrick. Kate felt a shudder run
through her which had nothing to do with the weather.
Why on earth had she painted him, and now of all
times? It was like staring at a ghost. She glanced
expectantly up the row of houses, hoping to see Cal
coming around the corner, but no matter how long she
squinted in that direction, his now-familiar form never
appeared.

Cal woke from another disturbed night of confusing
dreams and re-awakened longings. Sally and Kate
seemed to merge in his exhausted mind, as his sub-
conscious brought to the fore all the feelings he had
been quashing for years. It didn't help, of course, that
Kate's smell was all around him, on the pillowcase and
sheets which he deliberately had not changed or
washed. Feeling pathetic, he groaned as he levered
himself upright. *No running for you today, lad,* he
thought morosely, as he made his way slowly to the
bathroom where he hoped a scalding shower would
reenergise him. Of course, the solitude behind the
curtain of running water simply gave his mind the
freedom to run amok once again. This time it was only
Kate who troubled Cal's mind, with her wide smile
and gentle hands. Her eyes, so haunted when he had

first met her, had come alive during their time
together, and sparkled with an emerald wit and
humour.

"Argghh," Cal stepped out of the shower, feeling
totally unrefreshed. He wasn't sure how long he could
keep up the pretence of not wanting her, how long he
could avoid her company, which drew him like a
magnet. He knew she needed space to think, just as he
did, but if he could only think of her, then what was
the point in punishing himself?

Giving up on her painting, and ripping out the
disturbing picture of her dead fiancé, Kate checked her
face in the mirror before stepping out to collect Connie
for their morning coffee. She contemplated the mascara
and lipstick that she'd found hidden at the bottom of
her handbag. She couldn't remember the last time she
had worn them, and they were probably woefully out
of date now, but she liked the effect. Taking pride in
her appearance was a new thing. New to this morning
in fact, and Kate didn't let herself deliberate on why
that might be the case.

Connie appeared before Kate had a chance to knock,
clearly watching for her at the window. Captain
flashed her his tail and ample behind as he

repositioned himself on the sill, dismissing her before she'd even made eye contact.

"Morning lassie! It's a dreich day to be sure!"

"It is, very miserable, but we shan't let that deter us!" Kate tried to sound chirpy, when in fact her stomach was in knots.

They walked arm in arm, each with a walking stick in the other hand, down to the coffee shop, whose bright interior was a like a beacon. Connie rushed inside first, as was her way, and Kate held back, suddenly unsure of herself.

You've shared a bed with him for goodness sake, you can manage a hello! The internal pep talk was enough to get her through the door, where she thought she saw Cal's face quirk in happy surprise, before he hid it behind a mask of distant cheeriness. His 'customer face,' Kate guessed.

"Good morning, ladies," Cal stood beside their small table brandishing menus, making no indication that he considered Kate anything other than a customer. Her heart fell and she chastised herself for the hope that she had felt. Of course, he wouldn't want someone like her. Someone guilty for another man's death. She could feel the panic rising. Obviously, she had taken her anti-depressant that morning, normally enough to make the anxiety manageable, but panic attacks were the only thing that could override it, especially when they came on quickly.

"Are you alright there, lassie?" Connie, her quick eyes always watching, had picked up immediately on Kate's change of mood.

Kate could only nod in response, not trusting herself to open her mouth in case a sob broke out. Her heart hammered and she wondered if she was actually having a heart attack this time. Her breathing came in tiny gasps and she felt her senses begin to reel as the dizziness took hold.

"Get her some water!" Connie ordered, dragging her eyes to their host, but Cal was already kneeling down beside Kate, his arm around her shoulders.

"Hey, I've got you, just breathe remember, in - and - out, in - and - out. That's it." Conscious of the other customers who were unashamedly interested in the scene, Cal offered to take Kate upstairs where she could relax in privacy.

"No!" She managed to speak now that she had a slightly better control of her breathing. "I may be pathetically weak, but I don't need you to play the knight in shining armour every time I have an episode!" She bit out harshly. Of course, she knew that she was just projecting her embarrassment and panic, her shame that this was the truth of who she had become. But the hurt look on Cameron's face sliced through her and Kate immediately regretted her harsh words. To give him his due, though, he stayed crouched beside her, rubbing her back, but he no longer spoke any words of reassurance, nor did he meet her eyes.

Without warning, Kate stood, scraping her chair back and grasping for her bag and stick, not even having had a chance to take her coat off.

"Sorry Connie, another day," she muttered, before pushing past Cal and limping out, one hand to her chest, and still seeing stars at the periphery of her vision.

TWENTY-SEVEN

"Get after her, laddie!" Connie's tone brooked no argument, but Cal was working in the shop alone as Monday morning was usually one of his quietest times.

"She made it clear, she doesn't want me fussing, Connie. Let's leave her be, eh?" And with that he made his way back behind the counter to fetch the old woman's usual order, though the heavy gnawing in his gut told Cal he was making the wrong decision.

"Ahhhhh!" Instead of going back to the cottage, Kate had made her way down to the tiny beach, where rockpools and pebbles mixed with a small amount of gritty sand and seaweed. It was her first time down here, below the street and she liked the privacy the large sea wall behind afforded her. The waves crashed against the shore in front of her, drowning out her sorrows. Shouting her frustration into the wind, knowing that if anyone heard her they would think her mad, Kate no longer cared. Why was she so feeble, so pathetic? Why had she even thought a man like that would consider a relationship with her? Her vision blurred with tears, Kate sat down heavily on a patch of sand, not bothered by how wet it would make her wool coat or how she would pay later with pain in her joints. Perhaps she should cut this trip short and head back to Newcastle?

"Angus, can you watch the counter a while?" Cal couldn't force himself to stay in the shop even a moment longer. He cast a look at Connie who nodded her approval, and shot out and down the road to Kate's holiday cottage. Several minutes of hammering brought nothing. He looked through the half-netted window, remembering last week when he'd found her unconscious.

"Please God, don't let her have done anything stupid," Cal muttered to himself, alternating between banging on the window and on the door knocker.

Coming up the slope from the beach, Kate spotted the man outside her home. No coat, he looked frantic, jumping between door and window. She knew it was Cal, of course, she could recognise him a mile off and besides, who else would it be? Kate fought the urge to turn back and disappear onto the beach again, knowing they should face each other and put an end to this thing between them – whatever it was, once and for all – yet not having the strength to face it right now.

"Cameron!" She shouted against the wind.

He spun on his heels and saw her, standing open-mouthed for a split second before running the short distance between them.

"Kate, I thought you'd… I worried you were…" Cal brought Kate into a bear hug, pulling her into him and nuzzling his face into the hair plastered to her wet cheek.

Kate could feel his erratic breathing, mirroring her own, and she wrapped her arms around Cal's waist, snuggling closer into him. "I'm okay, I shouldn't have said what I did, I shouldn't have run out, I'm sorry."

"Don't be sorry!" he pulled back to look her in the eyes, "Don't ever be sorry, please!" And then he kissed her. A scorching, passion-filled onslaught that held all of his longing, worry and relief.

Kate melted into him, the heat from their joined mouths warming her to her core.

When he eventually made himself break away from her lips, Cameron said, "Let's get you inside and I'll build the fire." Taking Kate by the hand he led her back up the small lane and into the cottage.

The fire lit, they sat together on the small settee, holding hands. Cal was worried that Kate's face was still so pale, and he brushed her hair behind her ear to get a closer look.

"We should talk, Cal," Kate pulled away slightly, and his hand dropped from her face.

"Aye, we should, but not now, eh? You're still shaken, and to be honest, so am I. Let's leave it till later."

Why put off the inevitable? Kate thought, but she simply nodded. Her body craved sleep and painkillers, so he was probably right.

"I need some tablets," she whispered, as if the admission confirmed how pathetic she was, she wasn't sure she could hate herself any more in this moment,

"For my leg and my banging head."

"Of course, it's fine to take them when you need them, you know? It's not all or nothing!" Seeing Kate's distress, Cal tried to reassure her, but the light in her eyes had dimmed and he knew she wasn't taking anything in right now. "Tell me where they are, and I'll fetch them."

Pain relief taken, Kate could barely look him in the eye. She just wanted to curl up and slip away to blissful unconsciousness.

Cal tucked her up on the sofa with a quilt and pillow from the bed, worry lines etched across his forehead. He knew Kate had pulled away both mentally and physically and he didn't want to leave her alone. She'd made it clear she didn't want to be in his flat though, so he had a quandary. Kneeling down beside her, he could tell she was already dozing off.

"Shall I leave you to sleep, sweetheart? I can get Connie to sit with you?"

"No, just leave me." Kate mumbled, batting him away with her hand.

Cal did as she said, though he wasn't convinced it was the best idea. His whole body ached from his emotional turmoil, and all he wanted was to take her in his arms, carry her to the bedroom, and sleep with Kate curled against his body the way they had the other night. Instead, he shut the door behind him until he heard the lock click down, and hurried back down the street, promising himself he would check on her later.

TWENTY-EIGHT

When Kate awoke to the hammering on her door, she had a definite sense of déjà-vu. She hoped to goodness that she hadn't lost another twenty-four hours. Staggering up from the sofa, she realised that she didn't feel groggy or sick, so thankfully she mustn't have helped herself to any more pain relief.

"I've brought you some food," Cal said, as he sidestepped past her and into the kitchen, "Just some sandwiches and cakes, but I thought it might perk you up?" The hopeful look on his face softened Kate's resolve that she should take them and politely escort him back to the front door. Checking the clock, she was happy to see it had only been two hours since she'd fallen asleep.

"I'll get some plates," she said, seeing that he had brought by far enough for them both. *Perhaps that had been his plan?* she wondered.

Cal sent out a silent prayer of thanks that his excuse for a visit had been accepted. He certainly didn't want Kate to think he was checking up on her, though really that was exactly what he was doing. That, and assuaging his constant need to be near her.

They sat at the tiny table-for-two in the kitchen and shared the mini picnic he'd brought. Kate seemed ravenous, and he wondered if she had even eaten since her Sunday dinner with Connie yesterday.

Eventually, Kate spoke, "Thank you, that was very thoughtful… and for this morning too," she whispered the last part, not keen to relive the memory of yet again displaying her failures.

"Any time… I'd love to have lunch with you any time," Cal held her gaze, his eyes warm and expressive, trying to convey everything he couldn't say.

"Thank you. But what about the coffee shop?" Kate suddenly realised he should be at work.

"Don't worry, Cilla is always on hand as a backup! She's an angel, really!"

Having never met this woman, and not knowing her age, Kate immediately felt a pang of jealousy at the way Cal spoke of her. She tamped it down and smiled half-heartedly back at him.

There was so much unspoken between them, it made the air thick with tension – both the emotional and physical kind. Kate stood to clear the plates, feeling Cal's eyes on her back as she faced away from him. Without saying a word, he came up behind her and wrapped his arms around her waist. Kate knew she should push him away, this would only make the inevitable harder, more painful – but she couldn't do it. Instead, she stood, with her head resting back on his chest, feeling his chin on her shoulder, her hands clasped over his at her waist. Still neither of them spoke. After a solid minute of bliss, Kate turned slowly in his arms,

"Is this a good idea?" she asked earnestly.

"It feels good to me," Cal whispered back, before lowering his mouth to hers for a soft kiss. Not the searing embrace of earlier, rather a controlled, loving touch which made Kate's knees feel like they would buckle from the beauty of it.

Stepping back and looking at her more seriously, Cal eventually found the words he needed, "Listen, I know we need to talk, I just... okay, how about we have the rest of this week to think, till my day off on Friday, then I've the perfect place to take you, where you can paint and we can have some privacy. It's on the other side of St. Andrews, so maybe we'll pop into that town for a late lunch after?" He looked so hopeful, desperate even, and Kate felt a matching longing inside her. A tiny belief that not all hope was lost for them. Certainly, their physical chemistry suggested that was not the case. But wanting someone, and really wanting the burden of them were two completely different things, she knew.

"That sounds lovely, I'll come down at ten?"

"Perfect."

They stood then, in the small confines of her kitchen, neither wanting to part. Kate desperately wanted him to kiss her again, but he hovered, seemingly unsure. To end the awkward tension, she reached up and pecked Cal on the cheek, his stubble rough and familiar beneath her lips. He groaned, whether in pain or protest, she wasn't sure, but he cupped her face in his hands before Kate could pull away, and teased her mouth with his, gently at first and then with increasing passion.

Kate responded. What else could she do? Her traitorous body was as desperate for his touch as he was for hers. They pulled each other as close as their clothes would allow, hands roaming over shoulders and down backs, until Kate had completely lost herself to him and he to her.

As the old clock chimed three, Cal pulled away, just enough to be able to speak. His voice, when he did manage to form a sentence, was low and gruff, "Till Friday then."

"Yes, till Friday," Kate moved away to walk him to the door. It was either there or the bedroom and she tried to clear her head to make the decision. In the end, Cal made it for her, passing the bottom of the stairs and stopping just short of opening the front door.

He turned to Kate then, his eyes still burning from the passion they'd shared, his hair ruffled from her fingers, and gave her a delicate kiss on the forehead, not trusting himself to leave if he tasted her mouth again.

Kate shut the door behind him, and rushed to the window like a child, keen to see him as he walked past.

Catching his eye, she smiled as Cal flashed her a wink and then strode off, leaving her heart beating a mile a minute and her cheeks flushed from his kisses.

TWENTY-NINE

It had been a slow week. Kate had avoided the coffee shop, instead hosting Connie at her cottage twice, once for elevenses and once for lunch. The remainder of the time, she had spent sketching and painting, sitting on the bench in the harbour which was dedicated to Connie's lost husband, Albert. Kate had even ventured into the art shop on the harbour front. Whilst looking tiny from the outside, it was actually like a rabbit warren of little rooms and cubby holes, filled with papers, paints, textbooks, work by local artists, everything a budding artist could want. Sam, the shop's owner, was lovely, too, taking time to chat with Kate and make her feel at ease. He had recommended brushes and pastels, but more than that, he had treated her as a normal human being, laughing about some of the local gossip and suggesting the best vantage spots for painting in the area. Sam had also mentioned the Pittenweem Arts Festival, held every August, which attracted artists and tourists alike to the town, wondering if Kate would be around then. Sadly, she had shaken her head, telling him that she was due home in May, though the thought of returning to her home in England left her with nothing but a cold feeling of dread.

Finally Friday morning arrived. Kate was buoyed by excitement at seeing Cameron again, pushing away any worries – there would be time for those later. She had made her decision, and she hoped his was the same. Washing and blow-drying her hair, putting on a bit of make-up, she studied herself in the ornate hallway mirror. A different woman stared back at her, bearing no resemblance to the one who had arrived two weeks ago. Brighter, more alert, less dependent on drugs, Kate knew that nothing and no-one could 'fix her' – this was her, take her or leave her – but she desperately hoped that she was enough. Grabbing her coat and bag, she left quickly, before the nerves and self-doubt could take hold.

Cal waited outside the front of the shop, having already brought his old car round from its parking spot at the back of the building. It was making a strange grinding noise, he noticed, but nothing was going to stop him taking Kate out today to one of his favourite places. Seeing her coming up the road, she seemed to have a new spring in her step, her stick only lightly touching the pavement as she hurried towards him.

"Hello!" She said breathlessly as she neared, "What a beautiful day!" It certainly was, the sky was a light blue, promising more warmth than of late, and the breeze was so small as to be unnoticeable. It felt like spring was truly on the way and it matched her mood.

"Hello, you," Cal bent to kiss her cheek and Kate felt herself blush as if this was the first time she'd been on a date. It was a date of kinds, wasn't it?

"So, where are you taking me?" Kate asked, unable to hide the flirtatious undertone of her question.

"Ah, well, you'll see," Cal flirted back, "But I know you're going to love it!"

The car pulled off the road at a small wooden sign that said Tentsmuir, and Kate was grateful that they appeared to be reaching their destination. The car seemed jittery today, the country roads particularly winding and hilly, and it had set her nerves on edge. So much so, that she'd spent most of the journey counting to ten, controlling her breathing... all her self-help techniques. Sensing her rising panic, Cal had rubbed Kate's knee and turned up the radio, clearly hoping to create a distraction. After driving along a track they eventually pulled into a car park nestled in a dense forest.

"I love this place," Cal said, turning off the engine, "And I doubt there'll be many visitors today!" Certainly, the car park was empty except for three other vehicles. Grabbing her bag of supplies from the back seat and his own backpack, Cal helped Kate out of her door and they made their way on a footpath through the trees.

"Um, I'm not so good with hiking. Rambling even is too much..." Kate chewed the inside of her cheek nervously.

"I know, sweetheart, we're not going through the forest, just this narrow bit, then you'll see." He took Kate's hand firmly and they walked slowly together. As they emerged from the chilly shadows of the trees, Kate saw a wall of sand dunes ahead – thankfully, a path had already be worn between them.

"Not much farther," Cal whispered, stopping and brushing the hair back from Kate's face and dropping a kiss on her cheek.

As they crossed the summit of the dunes, Kate gasped. Spread ahead of them were miles of golden sand, with the dunes and trees framing the beach on one edge and the beautiful waves crashing on the other. It was stunning and she wasn't sure whether to laugh or cry. If she had been able, Kate would have raced over the remaining dunes to the flat beach and further, to dip her toes in the cold North Sea. Instead, she stood, frozen to the spot,

"Wow, it's…"

"I know, isn't it just?" Cal beamed, happy that his choice had been a good one. Then he led her to the soft sand of the beach, laying out a picnic blanket he'd brought with them from the car and helping Kate lower herself onto it gently.

"I have no words!" Kate said when they were sat together, she between his outstretched legs, resting her back against Cal's chest.

"Me neither," he said softly, tipping her chin with his

index finger so that Kate looked up at him, giving her the distinct impression he had not been referring to the view in front of them. They kissed softly, and Kate turned on her side to better angle herself towards him. It was perfect, or would have been, had there not been the cloud of their impending conversation on the horizon.

"Why don't you start sketching, and I'll build us a wee fire?" Cal suggested, giving her one last, lingering kiss.

"There's so much here, I could draw and paint for days and the light and landscape would be constantly changing!" Kate said excitedly, as Cal spotted a heron on the dunes to the side of their spot and pointed it out silently. He took a small quilt from his bag and laid it over Kate's knees, making sure she was warm enough, before leaving her to hunt for some kindling. Kate had never felt so cherished and the feeling settled on her like a warm hug.

THIRTY

Cameron read as Kate sketched furiously, they had fresh coffee from his flask and cherry cake that Cilla had brought him that morning. It was peaceful and blissful, and they shared the space so easily, touching each other's hands, arms and faces regularly to feed their craving for physical contact with each other. Cal often just sat and watched Kate's talented fingers create her art, and the hours passed too quickly. Neither wanted to spoil the moment by having a serious conversation, both still worried what the other was going to say.

As Kate got up to stretch her legs, revelling in this new-found feeling of peace, she grasped hold of the happiness which had been so elusive for all of her adult life, feeling the sand between her toes, and the salty air filling her lungs.

"Kate," she sensed Cal standing behind her. As she turned, Kate caught the look of awe on his face. He was looking up and around, so she followed his gaze, but saw nothing. Yet, there in his hand was a small white feather, "It floated down, above your head, and I caught it for you!" he said, struck by the import of the sign.

Kate couldn't speak, her throat had become choked with emotion and she reached out a shaking hand to take the fragile beauty from him.

"I was just thinking," she said, "about how happy I feel!" And with that the tears began to fall, sweet tears this time, not the ugly sobs of anguish and pain that she was used to. She clutched the feather to her chest, taking it as a sign. "Thank you," she whispered, to Cal, but also to the universe. God, even.

Taking in the scene before him, the beautiful woman who already meant so much to him, whose hand he held so carefully, Cal blurted out, "It's a yes."

"Sorry?"

"I've thought about it, about you, about nothing but

you, all week, and I want to be with you, Kate, whatever that entails. Please tell me you made the same decision?" He ran his fingers through his hair nervously.

Kate smiled easily at his words, "Yes," she thought it best to put him out of his misery quickly, "Yes, I want to be with you. Yes, I want to try. You've seen me at my worst, and if you still want me, then let's see!"

They kissed then, tasting the salt and coffee on each other's lips, listening to the waves which were the perfect backdrop to their own sweet melody.

The sun was already dropping quickly towards the horizon when the pair made their way, arm in arm, back to the car park. Their visit to St. Andrews was postponed till another day, as they simply hadn't wanted to leave their secluded nest on the beach and face the real world, but they planned to have dinner together at Cal's that evening. They had decided to take things slowly. No more overnight stays. Cal had Josh to think about, wanting understandably to get the boy used to the idea slowly. Kate hoped they could stick to that plan, she loved how safe she felt when she was with Cal and knew how hard it would be to keep some sort of distance between them. Never mind, that was a worry for another day. For now, her fingers brushed the feather nestled deep in her coat pocket and Kate let out a sigh of contentment.

THIRTY-ONE

It had all happened so fast. Going down the hill in the half-light. Seeing the tractor coming up the hill in the opposite direction, yet somehow in their lane, Cal pumping his brakes which wouldn't engage and swerving violently to the left. The squealing of tyres. The dull thud of impact. All so agonizingly familiar to Kate, who thankfully lost consciousness on impact this time. The first awareness she had was of the cold, too-bright overhead lights of the hospital cubicle. The hum of machines and talking in the corridor beyond her curtain.

"Cal! Cal!" she tried to shout but her throat felt dry and raw, nothing came out. She started to panic then, clawing at the wires attached to her chest and the canula in her arm, trying to get off the bed to go and look for him.

"Calm down, you're okay," a kindly voice penetrated her frantic movements and Kate turned her face in its direction. "We're just monitoring your heart and getting you sorted, lassie, but you're fine. You've got an egg on your head the size of the Tay Bridge, mind, apparently the air bag in that old car didn't inflate. Anyways, you'll live. Let us just patch you up, eh?" She carefully removed Kate's fingers from the wires and laid her hand down gently on top of the thin blanket.

"Cal? Cameron?" This time, at least, a scratchy sound came out, and the nurse turned her face to her with a fixed smile, but not before Kate saw the shadowed sympathy there.

"Let me help you get a drink for that dry throat," the woman helped Kate take two small sips of water before she sunk back on the pillow again, exhausted and scared, "You're in the hospital in Kirkcaldy. My name's Sheila and I'm looking after you today. The doctor will call in soon, now you're awake. You'll have to stay in at least a day for us to monitor that concussion and do a couple of scans, so I'll sort you a bed in a ward soon."

Kate couldn't have cared less about herself, she needed to know if she'd killed someone else. She was a curse on anyone who loved her, that much was now certain.

"Please, tell me," she whispered.

"Aye, well, he's in surgery now, lass, so I have no news for you. Internal bleeding can be a tricky business," the woman paused there, looking like she feared she'd said too much.

"Bleeding?" Kate parroted back, before turning her head to the side and vomiting over the side of the trolley she was on.

"Och, let's not get worked up, now," Sheila cleaned up the mess with efficient ease, handing Kate a cardboard sick pan and sitting her up, propped on some pillows.

Kate's hands shook as she held the pan in her lap, willing herself not to be sick again. Her head spun and she felt like she'd just been hit by a bus – which was close, except this time it had been a tractor.

"Are you his next of kin? We need some paperwork filled out," the nurse asked gently, her kind gaze penetrating the fog of Kate's thoughts.

"Ah, no, he has a son, but he's only young. His parents live up North, I'm not sure about siblings." It suddenly struck Kate how little she knew about Cal. So little and yet so much all at once. She felt a wetness on her cheeks and brushed away the tears, only to have Sheila hand her a wad of tissues,

"Your nose is bleeding again, lassie, hold that to it for a moment and pinch. Try not to cry, now, it will make it worse." Kate wasn't sure whether the nurse meant the situation or the nosebleed. Either way, crying wouldn't help.

"I need to see him. As soon as he's out of theatre, please!" Kate grabbed Sheila's hand to emphasize her point and the woman simply smiled gently, neither agreeing to nor denying the request. She fiddled with the drip attached to Kate's arm and a strange peace came over her. The pain receded, her brain stopped trying to work things out, and Kate slumped back in a half-sleep.

"Rest," Sheila whispered, taking the bloody tissue out of Kate's hand, her nose now having dried up again. "I'll pop back in a while."

Cal came around slowly in what he later learned was the recovery room. His vision was blurry and he felt strangely numb, but he was hooked up to machines whose beeping jarred his fragile senses.

"Mr McAllister? Cameron? There you are, it's good to have you back with us!" A tall man in scrubs stood over him and Cal realised he was lying on his back on an uncomfortable bed.

"Where?" He whispered

"You've been in theatre, Cameron, internal bleeding after your crash, I'm afraid. Lucky you swerved and hit a tree and not the tractor! Never mind, you're alive, eh! Spleen was ruptured, we had to remove it and you needed a blood transfusion. Plastered your leg while you were under, broken three bones, just a few pins, all sorted now." The doctor spoke in clipped, practical terms, most of which went over Cal's head as he still had not heard the answer to his question.

"Where's Kate?" he repeated his request, anxiety building in his chest.

"Ah, I see, well, I do understand there was a woman in the car with you, but she is maybe still in A&E. We had to rush you straight to theatre when the ambulance brought you in. If you ask a nurse when you get to the ward, they can look into that for you." And with that he tapped Cal lightly on the arm, nodded, and walked off, to be replaced by a nurse who fussed over the machines and did Cal's observations.

"Please," he croaked up at her, "My son will be home from school. Please phone Cilla in my mobile to look after him."

"Ok, sir, your belongings and clothes are just here on the shelf under your bed. I'm not allowed to use your phone, but I can help you make the call in a moment, when I've got you more settled."

"Thank you," knowing Josh would be looked after gave Cal a semblance of peace, until his confused mind flitted back to the image of the woman imprinted there.

He just wanted to find out about Kate. He saw her through the fog in his head, at the beach, on the blanket – Cal was trying to reach her as he drifted off to oblivion again.

THIRTY-TWO

Kate lifted her head from where it rested on her bent arm, that limb having gone numb at some point when she'd nodded off, slumped over Cal's bed. She shook the offending appendage, feeling pins and needles come to life in her fingers and then some feeling further up towards her elbow.

I must've fallen asleep, Kate thought as she looked over at Cameron's sleeping form, his poor plastered leg sticking out and elevated above the mattress. Her head pounded despite the pain relief the nurse had given her, but it was merely a small irritation in comparison to the enormous relief she'd felt on seeing Cal alive and breathing. Kate had not been an ideal patient, she knew, having insisted on going to visit the man as soon as the nurses' station computer had a record of the ward he'd been taken to. They had made her come in a wheelchair, pushed by a hospital porter from her own ward on the floor above, but Kate had acquiesced quietly for once, if that was what it took to get her to Cal's side.

Shifting delicately to try to avoid the inevitable dizziness, Kate reached in her bag for her mobile, checking for any missed calls or messages. Earlier, she had found Connie's home number in an online directory and called the woman, asking her to check on Josh, worried that the lad would panic when his dad didn't return after dark. Of course, the sweet old woman had fussed and fretted and offered to take a taxi to the hospital with Josh, but Kate had managed to dissuade her. It was miles away, and night-time, and the boy needed Connie and the security of his own home rather than seeing his dad like this.

Kate stood and stretched her cramped legs, reaching over to brush Cal's hair from his forehead. Not able to resist, she dropped a kiss just above his blackened eye, shocked when he stirred and his eye twitched open.

"Hey, don't move, I'll get a nurse," she whispered.

"No, wait," he grabbed her wrist, quite firmly for a man so dosed up on medication, "Need you!" Cal looked like he wanted to say more, but the words would not come, so Kate helped him take a tiny sip of the water that had been left on the bedside table.

"I'm right here, honey, and Josh is being well looked after," Kate whispered, sitting back down and taking his hand in hers.

"You? Hurt?" Cal grimaced, and Kate didn't know if it was the pain from his surgery or the thought of her being injured.

"Just a concussion, cuts and bruises, very lucky. Apparently, thanks to your swift reflexes, we hit a small tree rather than the tractor – you saved us!" Kate tried to fight back the tears that were swiftly building now that she had him back with her. "But you, aw honey, you're in a bit of a state."

"Don't worry. Just need you." Cal's eyes closed again, as if he'd fought a battle with the need to sleep just long enough to speak to her. Kate felt him squeeze her hand and then go limp. Just to be sure, she buzzed for a nurse, wanting to confirm it was just tiredness or medication and not some kind of relapse from the surgery.

They tried to persuade Kate back to her own bed, but she was determined to stay with Cal, so in the end the nurses left her to it, with the condition that she would let them do her observations regularly and tell them when she needed pain relief. For most of the night, she sat watching Cal's chest, his even breathing making it rise and fall. The tiny feather had survived in her coat pocket, and Kate nestled it in her palm, hoping for some kind of reassurance or comfort, a word from above, anything.

Kate couldn't find rest of her own, try as she might, because of the thoughts which filled her head and gave her no respite. Her rational mind knew that she hadn't caused the accident – either of the accidents, in fact – but her anxious, paranoid, self-hating side told her that Cal was better off without her. She alternated between the two ways of reasoning, like a pendulum caught in perpetual motion. It was exhausting. Eventually, she found herself praying, not a conscious action, more a kind of muscle memory from her previous life. She poured her heart out silently, praying for herself, for Cal, healing for them both, to know whether she should leave him to his life, which had been peaceful without her, for the strength to do that, and so it went on.

As the light began to filter through the thin hospital

curtains, a knock on the door revealed an older man and woman, very well dressed, and seemingly a little surprised to find a woman holding their son's hand.

"Ah, good morning," the woman whispered, speaking to Kate but looking anxiously at the man on the bed, "I'm Alice McAllister." Her legs propelled her to the other side of the bed, where she picked up Cal's hand and kissed him on the cheek.

"Gordon McAllister," the large man offered his hand formally and Kate gave it a brief shake. She felt thoroughly uncomfortable now, out of place, like she had no right to be in the room, and stood to leave.

"No, sit down, lass," Cal's dad had a friendly but firm tone that Kate didn't want to disobey. Nevertheless, she remained standing, hovering between the chair and the bedside.

"The doctors gave us a brief catch up, but has he not woken up yet since the surgery?" Alice McAllister was pale in the dim light, large shadows under her eyes signs of a night of worry and travelling.

"He has, yes, once after the general anaesthetic wore off in recovery, and once a few hours ago here," Kate whispered, "I'm Kate Winters, ah, a friend."

Both women looked at Kate's hand which had seemingly moved of its own accord and taken hold of Cal's again. The simple touch seemed to make a mockery of the word 'friend', but no one made any comment.

Thankfully, Cal chose that moment to open his eyes, needing a moment to take in his surroundings.

"Mum?" he said, his voice raw and gravelly.

"Yes, son, me and your dad got a call from Josh and drove straight down. He's fine, Cilla and Connie are spoiling him."

"I'll just head out and give you all some privacy," Kate whispered, trying to extricate her hand.

"You'll do no such thing!" Cal turned to her, his expression serious. "Stay here!" It was the first time he had spoken to Kate with such authority, and she sat back down immediately, not having really wanted to go in the first place. His words were softened by his thumb rubbing gently against her palm, and Kate flashed him a watery smile.

"Mum, Dad, meet Kate, the woman I love," he said, trying to grin, but grimacing with the pain instead. Clearly the drugs were loosening his tongue, Kate thought, as she felt the blush rise up her face.

THIRTY-THREE

Kate wiped away the remains of milk froth from the coffee machine and smiled at Cameron, who was watching her intently. Despite it being weeks since the accident, she still would not let him try to work behind the counter, the heavy cast and unwieldy crutches making any movement difficult. Instead, Kate pampered and fussed over Cal at every opportunity, dropping fleeting kisses on his lips as she walked past to clear tables and telling him repeatedly and in no uncertain terms that he was not to get up.

Cal took it all in his stride, surprising even himself. If following this gorgeous woman's instructions and accepting her tender care was all it took to keep her happy, then he considered himself a fortunate man indeed. Unable to climb the narrow staircase to his own flat, he and Josh were now holed up at Connie's, who had a spare downstairs bedroom, so he only had the daytimes to feast his eyes on Kate.

As the last customer said their goodbyes and Kate turned the sign on the door to 'Closed,' Cal hopped up behind her and put his arms around her waist.

"We make a great team," he whispered, "You doing all the work and me watching!"

"Hey, cheeky!" Kate spun in his embrace and planted a quick kiss on his lips, sidestepping him to go and finish the last of the clearing up.

"Oy, not so fast lass!" Cal refused to let go of her and Kate huffed in mock annoyance, whilst happily accepting the longer, more intense kiss which he offered. Pulling away and sighing, she whispered,

"I love you, Cal"

"I love you too, sweetheart, will you go on a date with me?"

"A date? We're together in this shop every day!" Kate laughed, stopping when she saw his face was suddenly very serious, "Of course, honey, that would be lovely. When?"

"Tomorrow. It's Friday so Cilla will be in here. I can't drive, but I thought we could have a picnic here, on the beach?" Cal seemed so hesitant all of a sudden and Kate felt a rush to reassure him, running her finger along his stubbled jaw,

"Perfect, I'm doing some housework at Connie's in the morning – you boys make such a mess! – and then we can go."

"I can clear up after myself! I'll do the chores and collect you at eleven. Deal?"

"Deal." And they kissed again to seal the agreement.

There were no April showers the following day, in fact it was unseasonably warm, allowing people to walk outside without their coats for the first time that spring. The light across the Firth of Forth dazzled as it bounced off the water, and the city of Edinburgh stood on the bank opposite, way in the distance. Kate looked forward to visiting there when Cal was better, imagining the hustle and bustle which just a short while ago would have scared her off visiting. Since her own time in the hospital after the accident, Kate had been given a new pain regimen which had almost eradicated the need for her walking stick altogether, and made her wonder ruefully if she shouldn't have asked for help sooner.

The knock on the door came just as Kate was adding a hairclip to tame her wild curls and putting on some lip balm. Smiling at her reflection, she opened the door, trying to hide her surprise when she found both Cal and Josh waiting.

"Good morning, gentlemen!" Kate smiled and accepted Cal's peck on the cheek. Josh stood hopping from foot to foot, the teenager looking embarrassed at the small show of affection. He and Kate had become a lot closer since his dad's accident, both grateful for the other's company in the early days, and then becoming friends over family boardgames and Connie's huge meals.

"Hello, beautiful!" Cal hammed it up even more when he saw his son's blush, winking at Kate and ruffling the lad's hair, "Your feast awaits!"

They made their way slowly down to the shoreline, where Kate saw a small table for two had been set up in the shelter of the sea wall. The tablecloth and cutlery looked very familiar, and Kate guessed that Connie had had a hand in the planning.

"Don't worry," Cal whispered against her ear, sending

a shiver of awareness right through Kate, "the lad won't be eating with us!"

A huge picnic basket sat on the sand, with a bottle of champagne sitting in a cooler nearby.

"You shouldn't have gone to so much trouble!" Kate exclaimed to both at once.

"Nothing is too much trouble for you," Cal replied, his face serious, his eyes hesitant.

Kate wondered what had caused the change of mood, and accepted Josh's arm as he made a point of pulling her chair out for her and getting her settled. Distracted by this lovely gesture from the boy, Kate did not see that Cal had produced something from his shirt pocket and was hovering awkwardly.

"I, ah, I can't get down on one knee," he looked disappointed and perplexed, "I clearly didn't think this through…"

"Cal?" Kate suddenly realised what he was saying, and felt the emotion rising inside her.

"No worries, Dad, I'll kneel down and you can balance your bad leg up on my knee, so we'll do it together!"

"Bless you, son," Cal smiled at Josh gratefully.

Then, standing propped on the lad who knelt in the sand, Cal opened the small red velvet box he was holding, to reveal a beautiful solitaire diamond ring nestled alongside a small, white feather, "Kate Winters, I love you with all my heart. You have brought me back to life again. I don't ever want to be without you, will you do me the honour of being my wife?"

"Yes! Yes, a thousand times yes!" Kate needed no time to contemplate, as the tears of happiness streamed down her face.

"Thank goodness for that!" Josh joked, unable to bear the romance, standing up and helping steady Cal, "I'll be off then, now I've seen it with my own eyes! Thanks for inviting me, Dad... I'm happy for you both!" The last bit was rushed as the boy was clearly keen to give the couple some privacy, for his own sake more than theirs!

Cal took Kate in his arms and they swayed there on the sand, sharing salty kisses and whispering words of love. It was the ending neither could have imagined, nor even dared hope for. This ending that was their new beginning.

Epilogue

To Catch A Feather

EPILOGUE

Striding across the small beach, Phoebe Ross came to a sudden halt when she spotted the romantic scene ahead of her. A young lad, down on one knee, supported an older man's leg, jutting out ahead in a full-length, white cast. Before them, the beautiful woman stood with her hands clasped to her mouth in shock. Phoebe turned her head away, partly not wanting to intrude on the private scene, but also because it pained her to see another couple so much in love.

Her own break up of six months ago still fresh in her mind, the touching montage in front of her brought Phoebe's thoughts hurtling back to her own loss and regret. *Loneliness never hits harder*, she thought morosely, *than when you see others who have found their One*. Spotting the table set for two, Phoebe made the decision to walk back the way she had come, she was hardly in the mood for a pleasant stroll along West Shore now anyway.

Read Phoebe's story in

"A Stroke of Luck – Found in Fife Book Two",

Available from Amazon now.

ABOUT THE AUTHOR

Rachel Hutchins lives in northeast England with her husband and three children. She works as a freelance proofreader and editor at ITP Proofreading and loves writing romance books. Her favourite place is walking along the local coastline.

As well as her contemporary stories under this name, Rachel also writes sweet historical romance under the pen name Anne Hutchins.

You can connect with Rachel and sign up to her newsletter via her website at www.authorrachelhutchins.com

Alternatively, she has social media pages on,

Facebook: www.facebook.com/rahutchinsauthor

Instagram: www.instagram.com/ra_hutchins_author

Twitter: www.twitter.com/hutchinsauthor

OTHER BOOKS BY R. A. HUTCHINS

"Counting down to Christmas"

Rachel has published a collection of twelve contemporary romance stories, all set around Christmas, and with the common theme of a holiday happily-ever-after. Filled with humour and emotion, they are sure to bring a sparkle to your day!

"The Angel and the Wolf"

What do a beautiful recluse, a well-trained husky, and a middle-aged biker have in common?
Find out in this poignant story of love and hope!

When Isaac meets the Angel and her Wolf, he's unsure whether he's in Hell or Heaven.
Worse still, he can't remember taking that final step.
They say that calm follows the storm, but will that be the case for Isaac?

Fate has led him to her door,
Will she have the courage to let him in?

Both books can be found on Amazon worldwide in e-book and paperback formats, as well as free to read on Kindle Unlimited.

HISTORICAL ROMANCE
BY ANNE HUTCHINS

"Finding Love on Cobble Wynd"

A small coastal town in North Yorkshire is the setting
for these three romantic stories, all set in 1910.
As love blossoms for the residents of Lillymouth,
figures from their past, mystery and danger all play a
part in their story.
Will the course of true love run smooth, or is it not all
plain sailing for these three ordinary couples?

Lose yourself in these sweet tales of loves lost and
found:

The Little Library on Cobble Wynd

Considered firmly on the shelf, Bea comes to the Lilly
Valley looking for a fresh start. She finds more
companionship than she ever hoped for in Aaron and
his young daughter, but is heartbreak hiding on the
horizon?

A Bouquet of Blessings on Cobble Wynd

When florist Eve discovers that her blossoming attraction for the local vicar may be mutual, she is shocked when his attentions run cold. Could danger be lurking in the shadows?

Love is the Best Medicine on Cobble Wynd

An unexpected visitor turns Doctor William Allen's world upside down and sets his pulse racing in this tale of unwanted betrothal.

A standalone novel, with happily-ever-afters guaranteed, these are the first of many adventures on Cobble Wynd!

Available on Amazon worldwide in e-book and paperback formats, as well as free to read on Kindle Unlimited.

Printed in Great Britain
by Amazon

27493235R00119